The Adventures of

THE HUBBUB

D.G. Oliver

CW00848439

To my nieces and nephews: Claudia, Samuel, Olivia, Amelia, Jennifer, Louisa and even Edward. Hopefully, you might have a giggle or two.

Home Time

It was a super-hot day on the south coast of England. Rosie was absolutely buzzing to finish school and dash home. There was one thing on her mind, and nothing would get in the way. You see, she was a daydreamer. When she was younger, it was all about fairies and goblins. But today, there was only one dream for her.

She couldn't stand it any longer! She just had to get in front of that TV, biscuit in hand, to chill in front of Gammergirl347. Nowadays, streamers were the new fairies, on-trend dances were the new goblins, and little crafting ASMR videos were the ultimate Rosie pastime.

Sounds like a load of nonsense, eh? Well, maybe if you're an adult who stumbled upon this story. But for kids, watching someone else play computer games was the best!

Rosie darted out of class and sprinted up to her mum, who was busy chatting with her neighbours and fellow parents. 'Oh hi darling, did you have a good day?' There seemed to be a global secret pact where the world's children were only ever allowed to reply, 'It was okay', which is exactly what Rosie did.

Her mum, who was fully expecting this response, simply smiled and continued to chat. 'So we'll see you about four-thirty then, don't forget the charcoal'. Rosie's excitement came to an abrupt halt. With a rising suspicion, she was about to moan when her train of thought was interrupted by an enormous:

'MUMMY'

Her little sister, Pheebs, greeted her mum with a massive hug. 'Mummy, mummy, guess what?' she belted out whilst holding up her Star of the Week badge. 'Oh well done, Phoebe', replied mum, who insisted on calling her younger daughter 'Phoebe', not 'Pheebs'. Other kids were now running up to their parents, which was a chaotic sight.

Next time you're at a school pick-up, take note of how funny it is watching all the grownups struggle to hold bags, water bottles, sports kits, and musical instruments when the stuff gets offloaded by the kids.

'Right, come on then you two', said mum, who then followed up with her neighbour, 'See you in an hour'. Rosie was in full panic mode now. 'Oh no', she pondered, 'what's going on?' The three of them negotiated their way through the masses of people leaving the school gate and headed home.

They lived in a beautiful seaside community where the school was at one end of the road and the beach at the other. Rosie and Pheebs lived about halfway down, so they had the luxury of walking to school or the beach within a couple of minutes.

'So tonight, girls, we're all heading down to the beach for a barbecue with the neighbours'. 'Yay!' shouted Pheebs, 'I'll take my bodyboard!' Pheebs was normally as excited to hang out with friends as Rosie was about streamers. Rosie didn't hold back. 'WHAT? Nooo, I have plans, big plans!' 'Her mum, who knew their timetable better than anyone, had an easy response: 'Um, no, you don't. C'mon, it'll be fun'. Rosie was fuming, almost too angry to speak, almost! 'Mum, that's not fair. I'm really tired and just want to watch..'.

'YouTube?' their Dad interrupted. 'No chance'.

He had caught up with them from behind. 'I was waiting for you all by the school'. Despite having gone to that school for years, their dad still didn't really know what was going on, where to meet them, or who their current teacher was. 'What are you doing here?' Pheebs asked.

'Finished work early to pick up some sausages for the barbecue. Who's hungry?' 'Meeee', replied Pheebs. 'Not me', Rosie answered. 'I don't want to go'.

'You'll love it. Let's take some boards and have a little surf too!' dad grabbed them both by the hand and ran down the road, pulling them behind.

Pheebs was loving life, with a big grin and chuckling as she went. Rosie's frown tried desperately to turn upside down, but it didn't happen, so dad decided to run in a circle instead, pulling them both round and round until she had no choice but to crack a smile. It was either that or die from dizziness.

They reached their home, a beachy-looking house with one too many weeds creeping through the driveway and the odd seashell scattered about from Pheebs's collection. 'Right then', dad said. 'I'll get all the stuff together if you can go and put your swimming costumes on then we'll get going'. Pheebs ran upstairs, 'Woohooo!' Rosie glanced over towards the lounge, eyeing up the TV, thinking about what may have been. 'Rosie, you used to love an adventure before you discovered all your screens.

Let's have the old Rosie back, just for a few hours?' She let out a little grunt as she headed for her bedroom. 'Why was life so hard?' She repeated over and over on the way up.

Life was indeed hard, not to mention stressful sometimes, but it was also full of opportunities and adventures to be had. Rosie didn't realise it at the time, but she and Pheebs were about to begin what would become a journey they would remember for the rest of their lives.

One day, long in the future when they were old, each of the girls would sit down with their own children and talk about this story, the beginning of their magical, crazy adventure together.

57 Times

'Come on, you lot!' shouted Rosie and Pheebs's dad from the bottom of the stairs. 'Off we go!' It seemed to be a common occurrence, Rosie thought to herself, that it took at least 3 times of dad asking before she would move. dad, on the other hand, always said it took 57 times, which seemed a bit overdramatic.

Plonked on the side of her bed, Rosie didn't really have the motivation to start getting changed. She already knew Pheebs would be ready in her swimming costume, probably being smothered in sun cream downstairs right now. 'Oh man', she glanced over to her upcycled chest of white(ish) drawers with rose petal handles from the local antique shop, with the vague idea of rooting around for a swimsuit.

She heard the slightest of creaking noises and turned to see her elderly black Labrador, Pepper, plodding into her room with a little limp in her back legs. Rosie's expression morphed into a huge grinning smile as she said, 'Hey Pepper', jumping down to her knees to hug her lifelong best friend.

'Aww, Peps, you're a good girl', she said as the old dog laid down in the back right-hand corner of Rosie's moderately sized room, opposite her bunk beds with the baby pink duvet. Pepper had a thing for sitting in Rosie's room, it wasn't the warmest in the house, nor did it have the fluffiest carpet, but she sure loved hanging out in there with her best human.

Pepper was as peculiar a dog as you can imagine, even in her mad old age. She could often be found pulling funny faces with a twisted mouth or showing her teeth, trying to smile when something funny happened. She hardly ever walked in a straight line and would often make odd noises just at the right time. Pheebs was sure Pepper was just stupid, cute but stupid! Rosie, on the other hand, knew better.

You see, Rosie had always believed in magic and fairy tales. On occasion, she had even fallen out with friends arguing that fairies were real. How else did she get a £1 coin when she lost a tooth? Okay, she didn't believe that one anymore, but some fairies must be real, and magic definitely was!

When it came to Pepper and some of the unusual things she did, Rosie was sure there was more to it than just being a stupid dog. There simply had to be, she'd seen it herself. There was this one time when Rosie was young, maybe 5 or 6 (she couldn't quite remember), she was swinging on a tree branch in the nearby park when all of a sudden, she couldn't hold on anymore. She dropped and fell, closing her eyes, ready to hit the ground.

Before she knew it, she had landed on Pepper's back and was riding her like a horse trotting along. The lab bent down to let her off, and when Rosie said, 'Thanks Pepper', the younger dog made a noise that sounded just like 'yoursss welcomesss'.

'Yes, that really happened', Rosie reminded herself as she heard her dog vigorously wagging her tail, so it banged against the carpet like a drum from a marching band.

'Peppy!' exclaimed Pheebs as she opened the door to Rosie's room and ran over to give the old girl a hug. Pepper responded with licks to Pheebs' cheek, making her giggle and stand back up to face her sister.

'Dad says we have to go now! What are you doing?' Pheebs was an impatient girl and was prone to getting a little grumpy with her older sister, especially when there were friends to hang out with.

Rosie, who was naturally far more chilled and enjoyed taking her time, still hadn't started to get changed out of her school uniform. She replied, 'Okay... Okay', and placing both hands on Pheebs's shoulders, turned her younger sister around to face the door and marched her out of the room.

Walking back towards her drawers, Rosie grabbed an old red hoodie hanging over the front of the top drawer and said out loud, 'Oh, all right, I'll come to the stupid beach'.

Immediately, all the hairs on the back of her neck stood straight and proud, her arms tickled with goosebumps as

Pepper made a noise that sounded just like ' Adventureshh' in a sort of doggy 'harrumph' type of way.

Rosie was completely frozen in fear and excitement, still staring dead ahead at her red hoodie. 'Did that just happen?' 'Did I imagine it?' With her body as still as a statue, she angled her neck around to look at the dog who was looking back blankly, with her tongue hanging out of the side of her mouth, panting rather gormlessly.

Suddenly, her mood began to change as she ran back to kiss her dog and started throwing clothes out onto the floor, looking for her swimming costume. Within less than a minute, her uniform was in a heap with her dress landing on Pepper's nose.

Her pink swimming costume with white spots was well and truly on, and her red hoodie was being pulled over her head. All that was missing were her flip flops, which, if you believed dad's 55th shout from downstairs, were waiting for her by the front door.

Hands Full

Laden with enough equipment for a 2-week holiday in the sun, the whole family set off for their neighbourhood beach barbecue. The girls followed their parents, walking side by side.

Pheebs carried her bodyboard over one shoulder, gripping it by the ankle leash and occasionally swaying on purpose so that the board floated out and clipped Rosie on the back of her legs. This didn't particularly bother Rosie, who was now in full daydream mode.

Despite the frisbee ring wrapped around her neck and a small cold box of sausages in her hands, Rosie was picturing a whole host of magical creatures down on the sand.

As she walked past neighbouring houses in their seaside-themed part of England, she imagined fairies in multi-coloured dresses skimming over the beach, as if they were seeing who could fly the lowest without crashing.

There was a huge, friendly-looking green dragon overhead, the size of a jumbo jet. Mermaids were hopping in and out of the sea, then a humungous sea snake appeared, opening its mouth to swallow the mermaids whole. Lucky for them, Pheebs interrupted her dream.

'Come on', she squealed as she grabbed Rosie by the arm and pulled her back to reality. 'Why are you always behind?' Rosie frowned back at her little sister, letting out a seriously grumpy sigh as she quickened her pace, breaking out into a little trot.

The family headed down the gentle slope to the sand below, the tide was quite high, revealing about as much sand as the length of a tennis court. 'Claudia! Claudia!' screamed Pheebs as she spotted one of her BFFs unloading a blue bucket and spade combo that looked way too big for her.

All the locals tended to pitch up close to where the promenade finished, and the sand began, as if it was their spot of beach just because they lived the closest.

Rosie wasn't the most confident in her group of friends, not often shy, just not always that interested. Deep down she loved hanging out with her friends when the mood was right, but more often than not, her imagination was simply the better choice.

There was a group of Rosie's classmates already running towards the shoreline. She considered heading off to join them for just a split second before reminding herself that she had better check in with those mermaids. Grabbing a towel off her chattering mum, Rosie carefully laid it out, patting it as she went to smooth out any uncomfortable bumps.

She lay down on her front, facing away from the sea to avoid the distraction that seeing her friends would no doubt bring. Resting her head in her hands, she gazed up and watched a pair of seagulls circling high above the roof of a tall beach-side house.

Following the birds as they went round and round was making her a little sleepy, but she managed to put that idea to one side! The thought of how those mermaids might escape the jaws of the sea snake occupied her mind. She gently closed her eyes, letting out a relaxed breath when WACK! An overly pumped-up football bonked into her head as painfully as anything she could remember.

Now then, a strange thing happens when two of life's little creations come together, and these are dads and

Barbeques. You see, as sure as the sun meets the sky each day, other relationships in the world are inevitable too, and yes, 'inevitable' is a big word, but it really is the only way to describe the fact you are about to read!

When a Barbeque is started, lit, fired up, or ignited, any dads within sniffing distance will form a tight group around the flames and talk rubbish until the last sausage is served.

Our group of neighbourhood friends were no exception to this law of nature. Sure enough, as the first group formed, Rosie's dad reacted.

'Rosie, grab those tools, will you?' he said, pushing down on his bucket Barbeque to wedge it into the sand below. Rosie slowly moved up to her feet, staggering a little from the football blow, which apparently no one had seen, or if they had, they didn't seem to care.

She picked up the set of cooking tools from the pile of stuff her mum was busy arranging on a picnic rug.
'Here you go Dad', she mumbled, handing over the tools as she turned toward the nearby sand dunes.

Rosie had very fond memories of the sand dunes, she would often run through them with her little sister and dad, jumping over gaps between the bumps or tumbling down the bigger dunes. Her favourite was when no one else had walked on them all day and the fresh sand was so inviting to jump into from the peak of a dune.

She hopped up onto the nearest dune, leaving a chunky footprint on the way up. She landed on top of the mound, wondering how grass grew so well on sand dunes.

The sandy lump she was perched on was a particularly grassy one, it looked like a bald man with a spikey hairy patch at the very top. Giggling to herself, she leapt off one foot onto a smaller, flatter dune.

Glancing over her shoulder, she noticed her sister and friends waving and calling for her to join them. A few of them were swimming now, splashing about on bodyboards with two of the neighbours in an inflatable kayak. Rosie waved back and mouthed that she would be over in a minute.

She swung back around, preparing herself for the next leap when she suddenly noticed a little spray of sand flung up from over the peak of the opposite dune. She paused, looking suspiciously at the area, as if anticipating it might happen again. Sure enough, it did, like a puff of smoke rising and dropping, and there again, another one, and another.

Tepidly, she wandered around the side of the tiny hill, which was no higher than her knees, sat down and stared in disbelief as an enormous red crab, with what looked like orange claws, was digging its way down.

The crab had two round eyes the size of tennis balls on stalks, and if they hadn't disappeared into the sand so quickly, she would have sworn that they had rather striking black eyelashes!

Rosie turned her head as fast as she could, hoping someone else was nearby and had seen the crab. She leapt up, waving down to the groups of parents and over to the other kids. No one was paying attention. She started spinning around in a circle, desperately looking for someone, anyone at all.

Something Strange

'Rosie! Rosie! C'mon, look!' came the cry from the shoreline. Pheebs was sitting inside the inflatable kayak, beached on the sand, looking sorry for herself. 'I need you, hurry up'. Rosie noticed some of the other kids had paddled out much further than usual and guessing her little sister had been ditched with the 2-person kayak, she started running down.

'You're way too small to use this, silly', came Rosie's first comment, still panting from the short run. 'That's why I need your help. Get in and start paddling', Pheebs blurted back in a panic. 'The guys saw something in the sea. Let's go'.

'What do you mean they saw something?'

'Not sure, but they got excited, jumped on all the bodyboards, and started paddling out'.

'Argh, fine, okay'. Rosie grabbed the paddles from the nearby sand and pushed the kayak into the perfectly calm sea, hopping into the back.

Progress was slow, with Rosie doing all the paddling by herself, she was the more athletic of the two, while Pheebs was screaming out to their friends, 'Wait for us!' and 'We're coming!', desperately hoping to slow them down before they got to the good stuff, whatever the good stuff was. Puffing her heart out, Rosie got her little sis in amongst the other kids who had formed a makeshift circle of floating children around what looked like a strange glow coming from below the surface of the water.

'What the heck is that?' said Pheebs to no one in particular. All the others seemed to be in a kind of hypnotic state, staring silently down, bobbing very gently on the surface.

Rosie was leaning as far over the side of their kayak as she could to get a better look. The boat was becoming unbalanced as she shifted both her legs onto one side. 'Wow, what on earth?' echoed Rosie in a whisper, turning to meet her sister's gaze.

The glow was getting brighter and more colourful, a sort of bluey-green tinge which soon became a striking purple. The radiance became a solid light, and the light became a pulse, a hypnotic movement from deep in the depths up to the surface, pulsating like a heartbeat every few seconds.

As the illumination hit the surface, it seemed to spread for a second, surrounding the children and then disappearing back into the deep before the next pulse streaked into life. Rosie thought the whole thing looked like a light show she'd seen at concerts on TV.

The aquatic performance was very pretty and not scary at all, unlike what you might expect seeing a pulsating light in the middle of the sea. From the corner of her eye, Rosie thought she saw something move down below, temporarily lit up by the glow.

It looked a lot like the side of a mermaid's tail, but it was only a quick glance. She needed a better look! She slowly got to her feet, holding onto both sides of the kayak, wobbling the boat a little more than she was hoping. 'What are you doing, Rosie? Sit down, it's dangerous, Pheebs cautioned.

'It's fine, I have balance. I just want to see what's going on down there. I think I saw something, something you won't believe'.

'ROSIE – SIT DOWN!' came the angry reply.

But before either of the sisters could shout out for help, the kayak capsized, throwing them both directly out into the watery glow.

Trip of a lifetime

The girls found themselves gently spiralling around on opposite sides of a whirlpool. They weren't scared or panicking from being underwater, but instead, they were smiling and laughing as they spun around. Rosie thought it was a little odd that they could still breathe normally but didn't question it too much for fear of what the alternative would be.

Pheebs, on the other hand, seemed blissfully unaware that she ought to be struggling for air as she caught Rosie's eye and giggled uncontrollably.

Rosie peered up to the surface and concluded that they were about her own height deep down in the water. She could see the faint outlines of the other kids bobbing away up there, somehow feeling that they were a world away, in a different place altogether. She felt her stomach lurch and caught the expression on her sister's face – the whirlpool was getting faster, an expression that was somewhere between joy and panic, just like a rollercoaster.

The sensation of spinning was growing stronger now, and the girls were pushed back against an invisible wall of water, barely able to recognise each other's faces as they began to blur with the speed of whirling. All of a sudden, the turquoise light was back, pulsating up the whirlpool but much quicker than before – two or three times a second, shooting past the girls and engulfing them both in a bright and beautiful effect.

The girls couldn't see each other at all now, the combination of speed and light was becoming less fun by the second. At that moment, Rosie started to let the fear creep from her mind to her voice, but the scream was instantly silenced as the girls suddenly dropped. They slid down opposite sides of the whirlpool, like an enormous free-fall water slide.

After a second or two of sheer dive, the sides began to lean in towards the centre like a giant funnel, encouraging Pheebs to shout 'weee' as the walls caught them, gradually slowing the sisters as they curved inwards. Thankfully, the whole ordeal was becoming enjoyable again.

Precisely as Rosie's terrorised face began to form a smile, she diverted into a puzzled look. Directly to her left-hand side, that curious crab from the beach was sliding down next to her, although now she sat with a mini green crocodile rubber ring around her waist.

'Hello again', she shouted, 'lovely day for it!'. She grabbed both sides of her ring and ducked down into a more streamlined position. Oddly, this gave the crab a huge burst of acceleration, and she sped off down the side, soon out of sight.

The girls could tell the slide/drop/fall/whirlpool (all of these phrases apply) was coming to an end as they both entered a giant bowl shape from opposite sides, flying around and around, trying to grab each other's hands as they passed. Amusingly it was like they were zooming around a giant toilet.

They were losing both speed and height as they eventually met near the bottom of the bowl, eyes meeting as they fell through the circular hole at the base, directly into a child's paddling pool full of small, coloured balls, causing them to overflow and roll off in all directions.

'What the he'.. began Pheebs but was quickly interrupted by Rosie with 'shh don't say that it's rude'.

'Heck' completed Pheebs with a look of satisfaction – 'What just happened? Where are we?'

'I have no idea', replied her sister, turning away and noticing the crab scuttling away, rubber ring still in place.

'C'mon', said Pheebs, 'let's chase her, she can help'.

'No way!' said Rosie, 'Don't you ever read? That's exactly what we're expected to do! I bet there's a tiny doorway it'll disappear through and magic potions with riddles. I think we should go the other way, away from the... weird crab'.

Gary and the glow worms

Rosie grasped her little sister's hand and marched off in the opposite direction. In front of them stretched a loooooong very old looking tunnel. It was dark and scary lit by torches on either side. Normally, you might expect torches to be large metal sticks with a bowl shape on top, surrounded by a sort of metal bird's nest to hold a burning flame.

They would cast shadows, creating the type of atmosphere you might see in a scary film. However, these torches were a bit different. They still had the sticks leading up the wall, but instead of a real flame on top, each pole supported the weight of... well, an earthworm, complete with two mini arms, two mini hands, desperately attempting to hold onto a normal-sized household torch.

'Umm', Rosie began as she glanced up, still holding onto her sister. As the girls walked under the small spots of light provided by hundreds of worms mounted on each side of the corridor, they noticed how the little lights were shaking on the ground beneath their feet.

Both kids wore confused expressions as they looked around the walls. 'What are you looking at?' came a tiny little voice from their left. 'Wouldn't you struggle to hold a torch if you were 0.3 inches long?' Another little worm, a few paces off on the right-hand wall, chimed in, 'All the same, these humans', it said, 'they think they're so tough with their big arms and legs'.

'Why are you up there?' Pheebs blurted out. Rosie gave her an elbow nudge, whispering, 'shhh'.

'Why are we up here?' came another tiny-sounding voice. 'Because it's our job, of course', replied a worm. Pheebs could see the talking worm gritting a set of mini teeth as it strained to hold up its torch. 'It wouldn't do for glow worms not to glow, would it?'

'I thought glow worms were actually beetles', Pheebs replied, still trying to shake off her sister's grip. 'Oi! Did you hear that, Nigel? They think we're beetles'. Nigel the worm's torch scanned across the floor until it shone directly in the girls' faces. 'Ohhh, look at... eugh... these two – funny little humans, these ones'.

'Now look what you've done!' said Rosie, halfway between a whisper and a shout.

'I learned it at school. Glow worms are actually beetles, and flying foxes are just big bats!' exclaimed Pheebs, looking proudly at all the lights, which were now starting to move towards them. Before long, the two girls were completely blinded, attempting to shield their eyes with their hands.

'Now she's insulting flying foxes. Dennis, did you hear that?'

'Yeah, I did, Gladys. My uncle Bernard is a flying fox, one of the best he is, and he's cunning too! Just you two humans wait until I tell him. His blood will boil. He hates bats, he does'.

'I'm terribly sorry', Rosie replied, 'my little sister is still very young, she doesn't understand'.

'Yes, I do!' said Pheebs, stamping her right leg as she spoke – a move she often used when feeling impatient. 'Firstly, glow worms are beetles, and secondly, normal worms can't hold torches!'

To her surprise, Pheebs heard all the little worms take a sharp intake of breath, as if they had all been insulted at the same time. In fact, there's no 'as if' about it, they had all been insulted at the same time.

'Can't hold torches! CAN'T HOLD TORCHES!' Rosie thought that was probably Dennis, but she couldn't be sure. 'Right! That's it! – Oi Gary, go and show them what we can do with torches'.

At that moment, all the shining lights drifted slowly off the girls to the back of the long passageway, where another tiny worm could just be seen. Gary was larger than the other worms, he was roughly as tall as a pencil. He wore a white headband and had tiny muscles bulging from both his legs and his arms.

As he slid slowly along the floor toward the girls, he was throwing his torch up into the air, spinning it and catching it again, flicking it around onto one finger and then flicking it onto his other finger, all while flexing his muscles at the worms high up on the walls.

Pheebs and Rosie were still a little way off, so most of this detail was lost on them, except that they could hear the chants and screams of all Gary's worm-fans egging him on. Some of the shouts were far too rude to mention here, but others included:

'Gary! Gary! Gary! Gary!'

And...

'Go on, Gary, smash their toes in!'

And...

'Send 'em back human-side!'

One particularly posh worm cheered:

'Tallyho, Gary! Give them a jolly good thrashing!'

'Pheebs', said Rosie, 'what's happening?'

'I don't know', came the reply. 'Let's ask. EXCUSE ME'.

'No, don't', said Rosie.

It was too late. A few of the worms' torches fell back onto Pheebs, and she responded with, 'What's going on up there?'
 'What do you mean, what's going on?' said Gladys. 'Gary's coming, and you're gonna get it'.
 'And who is Gary exactly?' said Pheebs, looking as confused as ever.
 'Who's Gary?' she said. 'Oi, Nigel, who's Gary? Oi, Nigel! ...Nigel! ...Nigel! ...Nigel! Nigel! Never mind, he can't hear me'. (Nigel was busy chanting Gary's name.)
 'Gary is our champion glow worm. He's massive, strong, and brave. You've got no chance'.
 'And erm, what's Gary going to do to us?'

'He'll batter you, obviously!' Gladys wore an expression that said 'what a stupid question' without needing to say it! She immediately got back into her chants and swoons, wiping her little worm forehead with a mini handkerchief.

Rosie considered their situation. She didn't want to turn back because it seemed like the wrong decision, and besides, Pheebs had wanted to chase the girly crab that way. No, they must go forward and take on the very odd challenge ahead of them.

'Right, follow me, Pheebs. We'll just jump over Gary and get out of here',

'Or we could squish him' Said Pheebs not really meaning it. Rosie ignored her sister and started off with a brisk walk, not waiting to see what Pheebs thought of the idea. The walk soon turned into a jog as Pheebs caught up, and they ran side by side.

All of a sudden, the glow worms turned off all of their torches and fell deadly silent. A single torch beam landed near Gary, and a little worm could be heard whispering, 'left a bit, Dennis'. The beam of light sharply moved and stopped. The champion worm was the only thing illuminated now. Although the girls couldn't tell, Gary's pace increased a little, and his grin turned into gritted teeth.

Luckily, the single torchlight made it much easier for the girls to see where Gary was. As they drew closer, their hearts pumped, a mixture of thoughts going through their heads. 'What if Gary suddenly grew to our size or bigger?' thought Rosie. 'What if he can throw that torch really high?' worried Pheebs.

They were just a few paces away now, still running and holding hands. The glow worms started making a noise of anticipation all around them – the type of noise you hear as tension builds before a sudden event. Imagine a drumroll getting louder and louder as they got closer.

A few seconds before they met Gary, they saw his little face shining in the darkness. He did look a bit intimidating, even for a worm. That sense of fear was soon lost when his little worm voice aggressively shouted, 'Prepare to get bashed!' quickly followed by, 'Wahhh', a sort of mini-battle cry as he lifted his torch high above his tiny head.

Rosie and Pheebs simply stepped over the worm champion and continued running, laughing a little when the thoughts inside their heads were silenced by the ease of what had just happened.

'See?' said Rosie. 'No need to squish anything'.

The girls could faintly hear a wall of tiny voices behind them, which sounded an awful lot like disappointment. In the midst of the general rumblings came a single little voice, 'Blimmin' heck, Gary! We've been planning that attack for years! Now we'll have to wait for the next ones!'

Gary's reply was drowned out by the other worms joining in the moaning, but he probably said something along the lines of how he hadn't expected them to jump.

Sock thief

The girls found themselves in a large cave. The opening was a perfect circle with massive, exposed rocks from floor to ceiling. Every rock making up the walls was perfectly round, piled on top of each other to form smooth steps of different sizes.

The smallest rocks were about the size of a football, and the largest reminded Rosie of the huge inflatable gym balls they used at school. There wasn't much order to it, either big rocks balanced on small ones, or small rocks rested on big ones. The pattern appeared to be random. Crystal-clear water ran down the walls in-between and over the rocks, slipping through every crevasse.

Shimmering light danced off the flowing surface of the falling water, fed from a hole in the centre of the ceiling. The entire room was a beauty to behold.
The girls stared in awe and slowly turned together, taking in the entire space.

'What is this place?' said Pheebs. 'I don't know', said Rosie, 'but my feet are soaked'. Rosie grabbed her little sister's hand and led her to the nearest rocks, they climbed up a couple, desperately trying to find a drier place to work out their next move.

They sat snuggled up on a step, both of them began to take off their shoes. 'I hate wet feet, it's the worst', she blurted. Rosie was often sensitive to everyday issues. 'I don't mind', replied Pheebs. 'It makes a squelchy noise', and she demonstrated by moving her feet up and down on the rock below.

Rosie had her left sock in hand as she started spinning it around, trying to shake off the water. 'I've seen Dad do this', she commented, turning her focus toward the other foot.

Suddenly, a tiny little hand, the size of a newborn baby's, reached out from a gap between two rocks behind them. 'Gotcha!' came a small, babyish voice as the hand snatched the size 4 unicorn sock out of Rosie's hand and disappeared from sight. 'Wahh? What was that?' came the first shriek from Rosie. 'RUN!' belted Pheebs, and they sprinted back down the rock steps toward the entrance.

As soon as they reached the doorway, a strange little creature dropped down in front of them. 'Halt!' he recited, holding out his hand in protest at their leaving.

The gnome-like creature looked mostly just like a gnome should. He wore a red pointy hat and had large brown boots, he even had the usual long white beard too. The only slightly odd part of his appearance was that, rather than the traditional coat and baggy trousers, he simply dressed in a rather tight pair of purple underpants.

'Hand them over!' he protested as the girls looked on, half in horror, half sniggering at the pants! 'Who are you?' said Pheebs with a giggle as she spoke. 'I am Booey! And I demand your socks! – all of them. C'mon, take them off'.

'You're not having my socks', answered Pheebs, and Rosie quickly followed up, 'Why do you want our socks?'

'I'm a sock gnome, obviously!' came the reply, spoken with amazement that the girls didn't already know. 'You will give me your socks or face the punishment'. At that moment, a splash of water from above landed directly on Booey's nose and dripped slowly off. He didn't seem to react, and he was trying his best to pretend it hadn't happened.

Of course, this made Pheebs laugh out loud, turning the gnome's face bright red with anger. 'Right! That's it', Booey marched up and grabbed the girls by the wrists, stretching his own arms to their fullest height. 'You're both coming with me'.

The girls faced each other, shrugged and grabbed their shoes and remaining socks. They figured that they may as well go willingly as there didn't seem to be a better option.

The underpant-wearing gnome waddled away, trying to lead Rosie and Pheebs with him. Given his tiny stature, he was being lifted off his feet every second step, but this did not seem to concern him too much, he was a determined little fellow.

The three of them headed out the far end of the watery cave, slipping through a gap in the stones the girls hadn't noticed before. Looking head-on as they had been did not show an exit, it was invisible against the background of layered rocks.

Moving around at just the perfect angle revealed a small doorway carved directly into the stone. Rosie thought this was awfully clever, she had heard about optical illusions but had never seen one in real life. It also occurred to her that she wasn't quite sure what real life was anymore, but that moment of thought soon passed when Booey interrupted with, 'Here we are. Now you wait outside until I tell you to come in'.

In front of them stood an old-fashioned countryside cottage, complete with a thatched roof, smoking chimney, and white picket fence. It had a beautiful old gate opening onto a path of pebbles snaking up to a wooden, arched front door. Over the door, and in fact, all around the house, green plants with red berries draped the old stone walls, making this cottage just about the prettiest the girls had ever seen.

A Silly Scene

Booey was striding towards the gate with purpose! His arms were swinging, and his butt was wiggling. Both girls had noticed that Rosie's sopping wet unicorn sock was sticking out the back of Booey's pants, just like how golfers back in the real world sometimes dangle those silly little gloves they wear out of their back pocket. Before Booey even reached his front door, it slammed open, and a whole group of gnomes marched out. Each of them was in different-coloured pants and hats.

Now, Pheebs always laughed at everything, but this even made Rosie burst out laughing. There were 9 little gnomes in total, marching in a line towards them. They completely ignored Booey, and he fell in at the back of the line in the 10th position. They marched together in perfect time, like a very silly-looking army.

Pheebs desperately wondered why they didn't wear matching colours. The gnome at the head of the pack wore a green hat with pink pants, and the second one wore a yellow hat with purple pants, and so on, with as many clashing combinations as you can imagine.

The 5th...6th...7th? Yes, definitely the 7th gnome in the line looked different from all the others. He wore orange pants with a yellow hat, so nothing unusual about that relatively speaking. However, the hat itself slanted off at an angle, barely fitting on the left-most spikey part of the head. You see, the creature had a starfish-shaped head, which was odd enough compared to the other little gnomes.

More surprisingly, his eyes were where his mouth should be, and his mouth was where his eyes should be. He had upside-down ears with hooped earrings, and a striking black moustache below his nose, which was placed where his chin should be. Oh, and his nose was stuck down with sticky tape.

The little guy's skin colour was bright blue, and he had one single long ginger hair as thick as a child's arm, which sprouted from his top head spike and dangled down onto the floor behind him. His sunglasses were tiny and would have barely covered one of his eyes. Unfortunately for him, they were sticking out of his right ear, so they presumably never got the chance. He jolted in pain as the regular gnome behind stepped on his giant head hair.

Now both Pheebs and Rosie were kind and polite girls, especially when it came to people who looked a bit different from themselves. They immediately stopped sniggering when they noticed that one gnome looked a little different from the others, as they didn't want to upset him.

They wore serious faces by the time the 10 gnomes lined up in front of them, ordering themselves into a row from left to right, directly opposite the girls, like a grumpy-looking netball team about to have their picture taken.

'We are the gnomes who steal socks', said the one on the far left who had led the line out of their door. As he spoke in his tiny gnome-like voice, he did a little bounce on the spot, and his hat fell off. He recovered it from the floor quickly, looking embarrassed as the other gnomes leered at him down the line.

He spoke again, 'I...we demand your remaining 3 socks for our collection. If you agree, you can leave in peace. If you disagree... we'll get you good', he raised his voice to a high pitch at the threat.

'Get us good?' replied Pheebs?

'Yes, get you good', repeated the first gnome, his hat falling off again as he bounced a few inches off the floor.

'The thing is', said Rosie shyly, looking at the gnome who had spoken to them, 'I was rather hoping I might have my sock back. You see, it's no fun walking around with one sock on'.

'Ooohhh, you did, did you?' wailed Booey from the far end of the lineup. 'Well, that's out of the question'. He took the little sock out of his back pocket and passed it down the line.

Each gnome examined it on the way down, often with sharp intakes of breath, eyes wide with excitement as if they were handling a precious gemstone. When it reached the talking gnome who seemed to be in charge, he proudly announced, 'I name this sock Sir Ralph! Second Duke of the toe-warming clan of Cheddar'.

Rosie recognised the word 'Cheddar' from her favourite cheese snack. 'A sock can't be a Duke, you doughnut', blurted out Pheebs before Rosie had a chance to process a sensible response.

'Yes, that's a fantastic idea, little weird Girl', said the lead Gnome. 'In light of new intelligence, I name this sock Sir Doughnut of the moronic custard clan'.

'And you think I'm weird', replied Pheebs sarcastically with a frown.

Further down the line, the one with the silly-looking head made a noise that can only be described as: 'wahh-eeee-nugnugnug', standing on one knee as he spoke.

Pheebs couldn't help but laugh at this despite her best efforts. Rosie leaned into her earshot and whispered, shielding her mouth from the gnomes with the cup of her hand, 'We need to get out of here, these guys are bonkers'.

'What are your names?' said Pheebs, finding some confidence, much to her sister's dismay.

The lead gnome took one step forward, shouting his name, 'Looey!' The remainder of the gnomes then each did the same in order, stepping forward to say their name and then back as the next took their turn, so that the whole ordeal sounded like:

'Looey', 'Cooey', 'Mooey', 'Dooey', 'Fooey', 'Wooey', 'Silly head', 'Sooey', 'Vooey', AND 'Booey!'

Both girls noticed that Booey made a point of emphasizing the 'AND' before his own name, as if he was normally forgotten about by the other gnomes.

'What interesting names!' declared Rosie. 'Nice to meet you! Can I ask you all two questions, please? Why do you steal socks? And what's with Silly Head?'

The lead gnome stepped forward again and struck a pose like a posh actor on stage: 'As for your first question, that's obvious, isn't it? How stupid are you!' All the gnomes did little laughs and jumps at this comment, apart from Silly Head, who looked thoroughly put out by Rosie's second question.

'We steal socks to give them positions of power! To give them honours and titles! No longer will we sit by and watch socks being oppressed by feet all over the Hubbub. We won't stand idly by while innocent socks are wrapped around stinky feet! We are on a mission to... Wait!' interrupted Rosie. 'What's the Hubbub? Is that where we are?'

'The Hubbub is the land in which we all reside! The world in which miracles are aplenty! The magical, memorable existence we all know to be reality! The Hubbub is the here and the now!'

Before the girls could discuss this, Looey continued, 'And as for your second question, how rude! How incredibly unlike a creature of the Hubbub you are! To question why Silly Head speaks in his native tongue is both naughty and - 'Wait, what?' Interrupted Rosie again. 'It was more about his unusual... Well, the way he... C'mon, you know what I'm talking about? The shape of his head? His nose is stuck on with tape for goodness sake, and he's got glasses sticking out of his ear!'

The second shocked reaction from the gnomes was obvious. They were all visibly offended, and Silly Head was shaking with rage, tears somehow streaming up his cheeks instead of down. Even Pheebs looked at her sister in surprise, mouth open and slightly speechless.

'I'm so sorry, I didn't mean to..'.

'I've heard enough!' interrupted Looey. 'Gnomes of the Hubbub, attack! And leave no sock un-stolen'.

The line of gnomes ordered themselves into an arrow shape with a bit of shuffling around and arguing about who should be at the point. After a minute or two, they gave out a little cry of 'charge!' (Silly Head shouted 'WOOOOWEE') and began jogging towards the two bemused girls.

Oddly enough, neither Pheebs nor Rosie was intimidated, seeing how slowly the gnomes approached. In fact, they burst out with giggles when Silly Head decided to attempt a forward roll during the charge, knocking over all of the other gnomes, creating a heap of colourful pants and mild swearing!

'Come on, Rosie', said Pheebs. 'Let's go see what's next'.

The Willow Tree

Skipping off still laughing the girls found themselves at the entrance to a dark, dingy-looking forest. The trees were tall and thick, stretching as far as could be seen in both directions. Rosie and Pheebs took a step towards a thin gap in the trees which opened out into a path.

The way ahead looked straight and true, it was longer than the girls could see, apparently never-ending. The path was flanked on either side by dense, scary-looking trees straight out of a spooky story. Branches poked out here and there, yet they sprouted no leaves. Occasional beams of light shone through the dense treetop canopy where leaves did seem to grow, but they looked brown, decaying or dead. The whole scene was extremely un-inviting!

'Right! Well, we shouldn't go in there' said Rosie who was super into films and books. 'If movies have taught me anything there will either be giant spiders, elves or worse in there, let's go back!'

Behind them came a shriek of 'WOOOOWEE' they turned to see a hill had appeared with Silly Head at the top roly-polyIng down towards them. Over the brow of the hill came the other gnomes still charging away.

'Come on' said Pheebs it's not that bad' this is real life, not a silly make-believe book! 'Hmm' came the reply from her bigger sister with one eyebrow raised 'I don't want to get run-over – ok, follow me'.

Rosie and Pheebs slowly ventured onto the path one small step at a time. After roughly four paces they heard a very fast, very sharp noise, the bending, breaking, and snapping of wood directly behind them. Both jumped around in horror to see that the entrance to the path had gone, and a solid wall of tree trunks and branches covered in pointy prickles had replaced it.

'Rosie, I'm scared' whimpered Pheebs, grabbing her sister's hand as she spoke. 'It's ok you've got this', answered her sister doing her best to sound grown up but beginning to shake in her boots!

'Come Along!' Echoed a big booming voice throughout the wood, 'I haven't got all day'.

The fear coursing throughout the girls subsided a little, in Rosie's case it was replaced with suspicion 'Who's that?' 'Where is it coming from?' 'How is it so spooky?' were the questions circling around in her head. Pheebs on the other hand began grinning slightly.

'What are you smiling about?' said Rosie

'That voice? We're safe now!' replied Pheebs.

'How do you know?'

'it sounds like Father Christmas...'

'it's definitely NOT Father Christmas, why would he be here?'

Before Pheebs got the chance to tell Rosie that the big man was chilling during the summer whilst his elves built presents the huge voice suddenly bellowed:

'What is a Christmas?'

'Ok it's not him' admitted Pheebs, 'but he seems nice enough let's go find out'.

Reluctantly Rosie slowly nodded. Normally she was the braver of the two but Pheebs seemed confident in her choice. Rosie glanced behind them again to check the entrance was still blocked, and the two girls walked on, still hand in hand.

'I have been waiting a long time to meet you' the voice announced. 'A long time indeed'.

Not wanting to reply for fear of what might come next, the girls continued. The never-ending straight path through the woods suddenly produced a sharp turn off to the right, Pheebs had thought it looked just like one of those 'right angles' at 90 something or other they had learned in Maths.

They emerged into a small opening, the path led into a slightly raised area off the ground with a squidgy floor of old branches covered in moss. Directly in front of the children stood a huge tree stretching high above the girls' heads. The tree had luscious green branches weeping down with leaves like green tears frozen in time.

Together the branches and leaves formed shapes just like umbrellas balanced on top of one another surrounding the thick brown tree trunk. The trunk itself branched off into two smaller trunks creating a perfect 'Y' shape of brown flaky bark.

'Hello there little ones, my name is Willow the wise'.

Pheebs leaned into her sister's ear and whispered: 'Wow did that tree just talk?'

'Tree?' the tree seemed to say.

Goodness no, I'm a puppy'.

Suddenly a tiny little, fluffy pup toddled around from behind the tree sitting neatly in front of the girls like a good girl. Willow was a small cocker-poo who had been neatly groomed with a fluffy but short golden coat, trimmed so that she had slightly more fur on her head and tail than her body.

One of Willow's paws reached behind her back and pulled out a voice-changing mega-phone which was small in the talking end with a coned-shaped funnel to project the sound at the far end. She held the megaphone up against her cute little mouth 'Like I said, I have been waiting for you' said the giant, booming voice.

'Hehe' giggled Pheebs 'that's crazy, you're soooo cute' and she stretched forward to cuddle the tiny puppy. The megaphone came back out, as Willow stepped back 'Willow the wise does not permit cuddles, petting, stroking or anything in between. I am simply here to guide you on your quest'. 'Oh... Willow' said Pheebs I get it. Like a Willow-Tree.

'A quest?' repeated Rosie, I didn't know we were on a quest! One minute we were paddling in the sea, and the next...

'Silence human child, there is much to be discussed'.

'Do you think we could talk without the voice changer please?' Responded Rosie 'We are standing right here, there really is no need to shout!'

'Yes, well, indeed said Willow using the megaphone for the last time and putting it behind her back, somehow hiding it from the children. Now speaking in a high-pitched, cute voice Willow continued, 'You see, you were brought here for a very specific task. A task that only human children can do and you two happened to be the nearest at the time'.

Rosie and Pheebs were a little taken-a-back by this, who would have thought that this adventure was anything other than an accident? or a daydream at very best.

'Long ago here in the Hubbub' continued Willow, 'there was harmony, balance! a yin for the yang, light for dark and laughter for tears. Presently the balance is gone, there is simply no' Willow reached for the megaphone 'equilibrium' she bellowed.

'Equi – what now?' repeated Rosie

'Equilibrium! means a calm state of balance' Willow explained 'where two opposing forces meet in the middle to create stability. You see sometimes life can be good, sometimes bad. If we were happy all the time, happiness wouldn't be such a joy when it arrived, would it?

We would be so used to the feeling of a smile that it would simply feel like every other moment and not at all special. For happiness to be truly meaningful we also need sadness, so we have something to compare our smile to. Do you see?

'I think so' Rosie mumbled softly,

'I do' Pheebs piped up. 'If I laughed all day long whatever I was laughing about wouldn't be funny anymore'.

'Yes... that's the idea little one, any living creature from a fly to a puppy needs different emotions to suit different moments, our brains switch us in and out of emotional states in a nano-second, before our bodies get a chance to join in and react, be it producing tears or bending our mouths into different shapes to show sadness, happiness, or anything in-between.

'So, you're saying here in the Hubbub the creatures don't feel happy anymore?' asked Rosie.

'Not exactly little human! What I'm saying is'..

'Hey I'm bigger than you!' snorted Rosie

'Even I'M bigger than you!' Pheebs added defiantly.

'My point li... sorry big humans is that, balance has been removed from the Hubbub, those of us that were happy at the time it was lost have stayed happy, of a sort, and those who were sad have stayed that way too. Likewise, for those that were excited, they have remained so and those that were nervous are forever anxious.

But of course, without experiencing the opposite emotions they don't even realise it has happened, it is a terrible curse, and one that must be lifted!

'What are we expected to do about it?' said Pheebs with one of her little jumps.

'Dear child, isn't it obvious?'

'No' Came the reply

'You must find the Snappies, and make them become friends again, only with this will the creatures of the Hubbub find their calm.

A Quest for the ages

'The Snappies?' they both repeated together.

'Yes, of course', continued Willow. Long ago, two twins were created, not born like you or me, but invented by their keeper'. Willow paused momentarily to check if the girls were paying attention, and then continued, 'The Snappies lived as companions for a great many years, always off on some adventure or another, with their keeper not far behind.

They were best friends, always looking out for one another and, of course, helping many of us Hubbub creatures during our hours of need. Once they helped me find my favourite dog chew, it was under the sofa!

Willow was staring up wistfully at the sky as she spoke, as if thinking of better times. 'To be honest, all we want to do is go home', said Rosie, looking at her younger sister. 'We have been here for so long'. Despite the situation, Rosie still managed to daydream. She floated off back home, remote in hand, watching some YouTube creator make shapes with slime.

'I reckon my hot dog is ready by now', added Pheebs. 'Probably got sand all over it'. Her dad had a habit of dropping sausages into the sand and cleaning them off when no one was watching.

'But girls, you see, this is your purpose here. It's why you were summoned here. Your path is laid out before you, and only by completing your quest will you be able to return to your strange world'.

'How can you think our world is strange compared to this?' said Rosie.

'We hear rumours down here, strange tales of prisons called schools, where your young are forced to sit quietly and raise their hands into the air before speaking to an overlord. Is it true that if the overlord chooses the young person to speak, it must be in answer to a question rather than a song, joke, or fart noise?'

'Well, sort of', replied Rosie. 'Although we don't call them overlords, they are teachers, and fart noises are for immature boys and babies!'

Pheebs decided to test this idea out and blew a massive raspberry, which sent Willow rolling onto her back, laughing. Rosie looked disapprovingly at her little sister as they waited roughly 2 minutes for the puppy to stop giggling and get back to her feet.

'Wait a minute!' chorused both sisters together, as if a giant penny had just dropped.

'You laughed', continued Pheebs. 'And earlier on, you were all serious and strict, shouting into that megaphone. How come you have your equi-wassit?'

'Ummm? Me? Well... I, I suppose I... QUIET! Silly small child, your quest awaits... now BEGONE!'

It's fair to say what happened next spooked the girls, Willow went up in a puff of smoke, quite literally. She shot up into the sky, tumbling and twisting as she went, faster than a rocket, and soon disappearing out of sight. A rising stream of smoke followed her skyward, as if she was being propelled up but somehow without a visible sign of flame or fire. The whole ordeal was very odd and forced Pheebs to jump behind her bigger sister as they both looked on in trepidation.

'W..w..w..what just happened, Rosie? I don't like it'.

'I have no idea. Let's go, that was way too sketchy'.

An oasis full of weird

The sisters turned away from the giant tree and ventured a few nervous steps onto what now appeared to be a cliff top. They were greeted with luscious, green rolling hills in all directions and more picture-book waterfalls than you could shake a stick at. The sound of falling water splashing against rock was overwhelmingly lovely. As their eyes scanned the scene before them, never had they felt more a part of a fairy tale.

Overhead, birds swooped and chirped pleasantly in great flocks. To their left, deer were running and jumping through the grassland. To their right, hundreds of ponies and donkeys stood around munching away without a care in the world.

The sun was bright and warming, almost cartoon-like as it gracefully floated high above. Oddly, the girls found that they could stare at it without hurting their eyes. As they did, a perfect rainbow appeared too, the colours stood out brightly and individually rather than blending in as you might expect. From red to violet, each had its own distinct line as if drawn by a talented young child.

When the girls squinted hard enough, they could just about see small fairy-like creatures running along the rainbow peak and sliding down in either direction in a joyful scene, just like the type of sight Rosie often dreamed of.

'Let's take a look over the edge', suggested Pheebs. The two of them peered down into the valley beneath. It was hard to make out much, what with all the waterfalls that plunged into the river and spray that bounded off the water like a great mist.

'What doing?'

'Hmm? Sorry, what was that?' Rosie asked.

'What doing?' came the reply, but this time both girls heard it, in a low, kind of musky voice.

Rosie felt the smallest of tugs on her shorts. Indifferently, she glanced down to see a very odd thing indeed, although nowadays she thought it not so unexpected. Below her stood a miniature dinosaur. It was T-Rex-like in appearance with two strong bottom legs, wearing red welly boots.

It had an upright torso and weedy little arms bent at the claw. The creature's head looked like the typical Tyrannosaurus from the movies: long, scary, sharp teeth – you know the type of thing, only much smaller and wearing a straw hat. The dinosaur was very short, its head was level with Rosie's waist, and she wasn't particularly tall.

'What doing?' it repeated, this time looking directly into Rosie's eyes and tilting its head like a puppy to signal curiosity. 'Oh, just enjoying the view', came the response from Pheebs as calmly confident as any child could, she didn't look in the slightest bit shocked. 'It's really pretty'.

'What is pretty?' asked the little dinosaur looking up at Pheebs. 'The view! The view is pretty, the rainbows, the waterfalls... the fairies, all of it, it's all absolutely... 'Nooo, not understand, what mean pretty?' the creature asked.

'Oh, I see, well pretty means when something is really nice to look at'.

'I is pretty?'

'Um.. yes, of course, in your own sort of way', suggested Rosie.

'For a dinosaur anyway', said Pheebs.

'I not dinosaur, I is Dino-Rex'.

'I suppose you're quite cute', continued Rosie.

'Please could you tell us where we are?

'We is at Hubbub, is pretty place?' 'Yes, yes, it is pretty', said Pheebs.

'Can you tell us if you know anything about the snappies?'

The Dino-Rex didn't blink, staring at the girls from one to the other, his head still tilting from left to right. 'SNAPPIES? He suddenly barked back. 'I is knowing of snappies', the mini dinosaur took a deep breath and calmed his voice.

'Sorry, not knowing why is shouting, snappies is friends of Dino-Rex, we is always playing bittings and snap snapings'.

'Oh fantastic!' bellowed Rosie, 'and can you please tell us where to find them? We need to help them become friends again, it's our quest you see'. 'S..E..A?' the little guy roared up at the sisters. The noise and force of his roar hit them like a brick, flung from a truck full of bricks, driving away from a tornado of bricks and crashing into the biggest brick wall in the brick factory.

'Huh?' wondered Pheebs. 'Sea Is very wet and full of fishys'. The Dino-Rex turned and began running off across a meadow of wildflowers, squishing them as he went, the footsteps of a tiny T-Rex were surprisingly loud, causing a crashing sound every time one of the dino-feet bounced off the earth. 'What the heck? Come on, Pheebs! We need to follow him'.

The two of them set off as fast as they could, just a few paces in, they realised that they were faster than the not-soagile little dinosaur. Luckily, he had neatly squished a nice path through the flowers to follow.

As they ran, they noticed all sorts of little fairy creatures fluttering through the petals surrounding them on both sides. Some had bodies of girls and boys with heads of lizards, whereas others had lizard bodies with human heads.

Up ahead, Pheebs noticed a small, grumpy-looking troll sitting under a toadstool. He was holding a broken old fishing rod, staring at it as if he were trying to work out why it was snapped in half. The troll raised his head at the approaching kerfuffle and looked more and more concerned as the girls gained on him.

When they were a few paces off, he sensed what was about to happen, dropped both halves of the rod, and hugged the plant's stalk - closing his eyes and gritting his teeth. 'Wahhhh! Was all they could make out as the toadstool took off, spinning up, up, and away in the force of the girls sprinting past.

Before they knew it, the girls were jogging along either side of the Dino-Rex, doing their very best to avoid bumping into all the flying fairies - who were themselves panicking and taking evasive action.

'What doing?' 'What do you mean what doing? – we are following you to the snappies', declared Rosie desperately. 'Snappies? Yes, is my friends, where is snappies?' said the Dino softly as he looked up at Rosie, still trotting along. 'ARGH' screamed Pheebs, 'we're never going to get out of here. All I wanted to do was play on the beach with my friends, we're never going to get out of here!' The Dino Rex seemed to suddenly realise something and interrupted with 'I take to snappies'. He accelerated off, faster than he had managed before. It must have only taken 4 or 5 strides before he banged his front leg into the log and went down with a violent tumble.

'OI!' came the shout from the pixie with the head of a chicken. He (or she) was sat on the offending log. 'Do you mind, I'm sitting here contemplating the fate of our reality'. Meanwhile, the Dino-Rex looked very sorry for himself, heaped in a pile of flowers, various fairies were busying themselves trying to help him back up and rescue the one he had squashed. 'I smash log', he sobbed.

'Sorry for smash, I hurt!' Suddenly an idea came into the little dino's head again, and he looked up from the ground at Rosie curiously. 'This one is pretty?' he quizzed while nodding his head at the pixie. 'Yes, very pretty. I love chickens', Rosie answered.

'I'm not a chicken. I'm a Pixie and a philosopher! – at least, I think I'm a pixie. I could be a figment of your imagination, or an NPC in a simulation game, or a conscious mind imprisoned in a body, or...

Wait! If I'm thinking this I must at least exist, therefore I'm probably not in a game. Unless I'm programmed to think I'm thinking. Actually, my mind might just be following a set of rules. In which case...

'Excuse me', interrupted Pheebs.

'Yes, how can I help? Or perhaps I should say, how can I help within the set of rules we both understand to be truth?'

'Eh?' Pheebs looked confused.

'Never mind - how can I help?'

'Do you know who the snappies are – and where to find them?'

'Oh yes, I know them alright- pesky little things'.

'We need them – would you please take us to see them?'

'Of course not, it's far too dangerous, but I can tell you where they are. I suppose you need them to go home, do you?'

Rosie stepped forward, right over the dino-rex who was still rubbing his leg along with several of the other fairies. 'How did you know that?' she politely asked.

'Oh just a guess, it's what they all say – normally doing exactly as that silly Willow dog told them to.

'What they all say?' repeated Rosie – 'what do you mean?'

'Nothing! Nothing at all' the Pixie was looking anxious as if he had said something he wasn't supposed to' 'Anyway if you want to find the snappies I suggest you head over there and through the tree trunk' He was pointing at a large, leafy looking tree with the biggest trunk you've ever seen. Smack-bang in the centre of the trunk was a round door with a huge knocker hanging in its centre.

On either side of the knocker were two perfect slits – cut into the ancient wood. The eerie looking door gave off an intimidating vibe and was certainly not inviting the girls to take a closer look.

Rosie and Pheebs's eyes met as they silently agreed that looked like a terrible idea.

'Oh it's not as bad as it looks' said the pixie pecking at a nearby ant. Having missed the ant by some distance the pixie looked over at the door again. 'Hey Doris, be nice!' following his gaze reluctantly the girls watched as the two slits widened into kind-looking eyes, and a smiling carved mouth appeared out of the darker wood beneath the knocking nose.

'I was only playing' the door said in an approachable voice which reminded Pheebs of her own Grandma, the type of apologetic voice she used just before giving Pheebs another present, trying subtly to apologise in earshot of the girls' mum and dad. They got fed up when Grandma constantly spoiled the kids.

'Come along children' the door began. 'I'm quite friendly you know, I'll help you get to where you need to go' Slowly the door opened with the sound of huge bolts being unlocked and the inevitable creak that doors usually had when there was an adventure behind them.

Rosie glanced over to the Dino-Rex who was nodding furiously. Meanwhile, the Pixie was gesturing to Pheebs with both arms pointing towards the door. The girls wandered over to the tree watching the door's face making little excited movements like an old lady when a cup of tea was being carried to her.

'Before you say anything Pheebs, I'm not sure we have much choice' Rosie said as quietly as she could to her sister, but before Pheebs could answer her back - the door swung open with such speed the gust of wind almost knocked the girls over backwards. A second later there was a huge sucking noise just like the dregs of a milkshake being inhaled through a straw as the sisters were launched off their feet and pulled headfirst into the tree.

Platforms and Peril

'Holy Heck!' screamed Pheebs as they landed with a bounce. Luckily, a giant yellow mushroom with white spots had broken their fall and bounced them onto a second smaller mushroom.

This one was hot pink in colour with black spots, comfortably big enough for them both to lie on. 'Oh no – what's happening now?' Pheebs finally managed to blurt out once the fear had passed a little.

They tepidly got to their feet for a better look, with nothing to hold onto they held hands scanning all around for clues about what to do next.

Although they didn't like to say it out loud for fear of being correct, it was frighteningly obvious what they were up against. The mushroom was high up, very high up! In fact, when they looked over the edge, they couldn't see the bottom, just a black abyss going down and down.

The mushroom they had landed on and bounced off was even higher, if Pheebs stood on Rosie's shoulders and stretched up as far as she could, then maybe she might just be able to touch the bottom of it. It was super lucky they had hit that one first and somehow plonked onto this one.

Ahead of them were hundreds of obstacles, rope ladders going at angles between bridges and crazy-looking zip wires which seemed to go straight up, straight down, or any which way. There was an occasional trampoline suspended by wires from above and balance beams that just seemed to float with nothing holding them up at all.

The nearest obstacle was a bridge the length and width of a small sofa, but others looked about half that size. In the distance, some appeared to be no longer than an armchair.

There was a chilly breeze coming from down below with occasional gusts of wind producing a white-looking steam as it rose past them to high above. The gusts made the slightest of sounds as they passed by, breaking the silence with a ghostly whoosh.

'I'm really scared', Pheebs managed to squeak as she shivered. 'Me too', Rosie quietly muttered, 'but we have to get out of here one way or another, and there's only one way to go'. They looked across from their mushroom at the first bridge.

It was perhaps a metre lower than them and a two metre jump across. 'I'll go first', Rosie said, letting go of her sister's hand. 'You can't! if you fall, you'll die!' replied Pheebs. 'Remember Sis, nothing in the Hubbub has been as bad as it looked at first – and there's nothing else to do, we can't stand on this mushroom forever'. She took a small step towards the edge, it felt squishy under her feet.

'Don't worry, try to forget about the drop - it's just like jumping off the sand dunes at home'. Rosie put her right leg in front of her left for a strong jumping position, she slightly squatted with her arms poised, ready for action. 'Ok, here we go, 3..2..1' She leapt perfectly, landing square in the middle of the bridge, both feet planted solidly together, but the momentum of her jump led her to put out her right foot after she hit the bridge, taking half a step with it.

All of a sudden, the bridge pivoted down with her weight. She thought her heart had stopped, as she leaned forward and looked over the edge.

Terrified, she put her arms wide like kids playing aeroplanes and took half a skip backward to regain her balance in the middle of the platform. 'Arghh...Oh no!' she shouted back to her sister, 'It's like a seesaw. If you're not in the middle, it moves up and down'. Pheebs didn't say anything for a while.

She just looked wide-eyed down at her big sister who suddenly seemed very, very far away. 'I can't do it', shouted she shouted with panic, 'I just can't'. 'You have to, Pheebs – it's the only way, I can catch you – don't worry!' Before Pheebs had the chance to continue the debate, there was a short-sharp bang directly behind her. She dared a glance over her shoulder to see a solid stone wall had appeared, shooting high into the sky above and deep down into the blackness below.

The wall began to move, creeping slowly towards her with a cranking, rolling sound like it was moving on giant wheels above and below. Pheebs let out a spine-chilling scream! 'The Wall – it's coming', she wailed, 'it'll push me off!' 'It's ok, you have time, it's slow!' Rosie shouted back, 'Look at me and jump, don't look at the platform – look at me'. Pheebs took a step back for a little run-up and exhaled a very long, deep breath, closing her eyes for maximum concentration.

'You can do this!' Shouted Rosie. She opened her eyes, not looking back at the wall, which had just reached the opposite side of the mushroom and was somehow moving right through it like it was transparent.

It occurred to Rosie, who could see a little more from her position, that perhaps the wall might pass straight through Pheebs as well, but there was no time to find out. Pheebs sprang forward and jumped high, higher than she needed.

She fell into Rosie's arms, causing them both to stagger forward and the little bridge to nosedive again. Pheebs dropped to her knees as they both slid forward towards the edge. 'Nooo' Rosie screamed, sliding down and losing her feet over the edge.

Pheebs managed to wrap both hands around the bottom of the flat platform as Rosie clung to her waist. It was enough to stop them long enough to shuffle back a couple of steps and re-balance in the middle. 'This is horrible!' squawked Pheebs right into Rosie's left ear. 'It's ok, you made it', replied her sister, still catching her breath.

Rosie was facing back towards the approaching wall, she thought to herself they only had about 30 seconds before they need to move again. The next obstacle was a rope ladder, an arm's length away, then they would have to step over to and climb down to another, much bigger bridge which had a trampoline at one end and a giant jump over to a skinny-looking rope bridge at the other.

'We need to move – come on Pheebs', Rosie let go of her sister, turned and made towards the edge, 'wait, this is going to tip down when I move, hold on'. Pheebs gripped the bottom again and watched Rosie shuffle along.

When the platform tipped, Rosie extended an arm and grabbed the rope ladder which felt far too loose and wobbly for her liking. She moved a leg across and then climbed fully over.

'Right, it's ok, come on Pheebs you just need to step across. Rosie was nearing the bottom of the ladder when Pheebs reluctantly clambered on. 'This is the scariest thing I've ever done', said Pheebs as she began climbing down to join her sister on the next bridge below.

Just then a violent gust flew up from somewhere down below again causing the rope ladder to flap around wildly. 'Hang on' shouted Rosie from below. 'I can't hold on' she screamed back 'I'm going...I'm going to...'

Suddenly Pheebs fell towards the far side of the platform, Rosie ran and leapt forward, arms stretched out, trying to grab her little sister...she wasn't quick enough. Pheebs dropped feet first, reaching out for her sister's hands in a last-ditch attempt to save herself. Rosie covered her eyes with her hands as her sister fell – the scream ringing through her ears'.

Then silence...

'What doing?' 'Why is sitting on floor?'

Rosie uncovered her eyes and looked below to see Pheebs sitting on an invisible black floor just a metre below her bridge 'What the?' she asked puzzled. 'It's a floor, but it's black so you can't see it', said Pheebs, slapping the ground all around her.

Walking along the same floor towards them, the Dino-Rex was looking confused 'Why up there and no down here?' He said up to Rosie.

'Well, we thought that was a huge drop and we had to go over all these obstacles to get out of here - How did you get here anyway? ' I is going through mad, talking door too'. Another gust of wind shot past Rosie on her ladder. 'Where is all the wind coming from then?' she said, a little embarrassed.

'I is having windy pops', said the Dino-Rex, cocking up a leg to fire out another one. 'Oh for goodness sake', said Rosie, jumping down to join the other two. They heard a distant, faint laugh which sounded just like Doris – the round door that let them into this place.

'Off we go – see snappy things'. Dino muttered.

Tales of a nobleman

The three of them wandered off along the black surface. Pheebs was staring up, wondering why someone went to all the trouble of making the crazy obstacles when they could walk along underneath and skip them all.

'Because it's a test! And hilarious!' echoed the voice of Doris again. 'Hey, how did you know what I was thinking? You stay out of my head!'

'Come along, Pheebs, stop playing about!' said her sister, who was picking up the pace.

'But that door – she... read my mind, I was just thinking..'.

'Shhh, little thing,' Dino Rex took Rosie's hand in his. 'I telling a story. Once in time, there lived a big grumpy king – he was called Smidge and he enjoyed a big human head, legs, and big strong human arms'.

The three adventurers reached a little stream with stepping stones made from upside-down buckets in all the colours of the rainbow. The Dino-Rex began hopping across without hesitation, and the girls followed.

'One day, Smidge was having dinner with Prince Wonky Knees and Princess Jessica'.

'Oh, Princess Jessica is a nice name,' Rosie said in the hope this story might become a bit more normal.

'Princess Jessica is only a nickname – her real name is Princess slug-head'.

Pheebs snorted out a little chuckle as the three of them reached the far side of the river and stepped onto a spiral staircase, which was also completely black and would have been nearly invisible against the black walls and floor if you didn't know about it. They began climbing the very long way up, past layers and layers of the scary-looking obstacles they had managed to bypass.

'During pudding time, kingnappers snuck into the castle and kicked out the Prince and Princess, sending them on holiday. Next, they kicked all of the court people out. Court people are the people who help the king make decisions,' added Dino. 'Then the kingnappers declared that the castle was now theirs, and King Smidge must have new court people – new people to help the king make bad decisions'.

The girls weren't paying much attention to the Dino's story and were looking around as they stepped up and up the dizzying staircase. Relief flushed through them both when they realised how high some of the bridges, rope swings, and zip wires were.

'What did you say? I wasn't really listening,' said Pheebs as they finally rounded the final few steps, reaching the top.

'I said the story of King Smidge, he's still in the castle, a prisoner in his own home,' said the Dino.

They stood before a castle, the type you see in medieval stories about knights, kings, and queens. It was surrounded by a vast moat and towered above them with enormous stone walls topped with battlements. Directly in front was a drawbridge, slowly lowering with the creak of chains.

The Dino-Rex continued completely undaunted by the enormous castle. 'This is the house of Smidge, the kingnappers are inside. You're going in to rescue the king. The king will give you tickets to the snappy show, you'll make the snappies become friends again, and then you'll go home'.

Rosie and Pheebs simultaneously looked down at the little creature. 'What do you mean, snappy show?'

'You children really don't know anything. Every 14th Friday of the week, the snappies put on a big show for the Hubbub. It's very exclusive, not all creatures are allowed in. I haven't been for 47 Fridays. You rescue the king, and Smidge might give you... and me tickets'.

The sisters looked excitedly at each other, realising this could be their path to the snappies and then home. 'Right, come on then, Pheebs – let's go find this king. Are you coming too, Dino-Rex?'

'No, too scary – I'll wait here'. The Dino sat down on the rocky floor and crossed his legs, looking wistfully up at the children like a puppy begging for a treat.

'Okay. Let's go then,' said Pheebs, grabbing her big sister by the arm and marching onward toward the drawbridge. The bridge was now fully open and belching out a misty, steamy, foggy type of substance, mostly to add a sense of foreboding to this part of the story.

Both girls were very much fed up with the Hubbub, so they didn't really worry about walking through a scene that would be rather concerning in any other situation.

Inside the gate, they stood peering up at the giant walls that completely encircled them. Looking around, they appeared to be alone, with only a slight breeze kicking up dusty leaves from the floor.

'Which way?' asked Pheebs, not expecting her sister to know the answer.
There were various old-fashioned entrances dotted around the inner walls, some with great wooden doors and others just openings carved into the stone. A flock of black seagulls flew

overhead, screeching to each other as they shot past the far end of the castle.

'That's weird,' said Rosie. 'We aren't near the sea at all'.

'This whole place is weird, Rosie,' said Pheebs. 'Let's just find this Smidge guy, get our tickets, and get home'.

They walked slowly toward the centre of the yard. Ahead was a completely square building with four towers built into each corner. It was made from old-fashioned stone blocks, just like the outside walls, and rose high, but not as high as the outer walls and battlements.

'Ah, do you remember when we went to Dover Castle?' Rosie whispered as they approached the gate. 'I think these tall buildings inside castles are called keeps'.

'No chance,' replied Pheebs. 'Keeps what? It's not keeping me!' Before Rosie had a chance to explain what she meant, a sharp, ear-piercing voice interrupted them.

'You again!' came a call from high above, on the front left tower of the keep.

'Who's there?' Pheebs shouted back, squinting to look up as apparently, a sun was now rising in the distance.

Yes, I say "a sun" rather than "the sun" as we simply don't know where the Hubbub is in the universe, I suppose it may be our sun, but then again, it may not. Anyway – back to the story.

'Don't you play dumb with me, little girl, you know exactly who I am!'

'Do I?' The penny dropped as the glaring sun moved behind a waffle-shaped cloud. 'Uh oh,' said Rosie, who turned to her sister and began to whisper in her ear. 'It's that gnome who stole your sock earlier. Yes, yes, I know, I can see him now'.

'Oi, Looey! Or is it Booey? I don't care, give me my sock back!'

'Your sock? Don't be absurd. Sir Doughnut is safely at court, helping to advise his king in kingly matters. Are you here to offer up your remaining socks to the noble life?' Rosie and Pheebs decided to ignore the little gnome, who was still leaning over the battlements glaring down at them.

They entered the keep through its main gate, which was one of those portcullis-type affairs – essentially, a giant metal barrier that could be lifted up into the tower itself.

Crazy Town

As they entered the keep, they were presented with a bustling town centre full of hustle and bustle. There were green shops, pink shops, shops of every shape and size. They saw a rainbow-coloured fish restaurant shaped like a giant octopus, a bright orange shop selling oranges, rows and rows of market stalls with all sorts of produce – everything from flowers to vegan spectacles, and even one stall selling upside-down frisbees.

Pouring out of shops, into cafes, and wandering around were a huge variety of creatures in all different shapes, sizes, colours, and styles of walking. Some used two legs in the human way, others hopped on bare toes, some favoured the roly-poly, while some stood still, looking confused at those who were managing to move about at all.

The place seemed huge to Rosie and Pheebs, far larger than they assumed would be behind the walls of the keep. In fact, Pheebs – who curiously looked from left to right – noticed that she couldn't see the four surrounding walls anymore.

All she could see was a busy place full of interesting people. She was desperately looking around for a human, but no, she had no luck. There were fairies, goblins, trolls, gnomes, and soldiers who had crocodile heads and puppy legs with no torso to speak of, just a spear and a pointy metal helmet. She also noticed giant snakes in all sorts of patterns slithering around with moustaches and beanie hats.

'You there, little girl', came a shout above the noise of all the commotion. Pheebs looked up to see a very tall and skinny old lady troll looking down on them from behind her stall. Despite being a troll, she looked nice enough, with her huge smile, straw hat, and blue dungarees.

'What's your favourite animal, little one?' she said, spreading out her hands to reveal a market stall full of cuddly, soft toys.

'I like elephants', said Pheebs, looking round to check if Rosie was still standing next to her.

'Then an elephant it shall be – do you like the minty ones or the standard grey type? – In fact, never mind, we'll go for a normal one'. The troll clapped her hands three times, creating a pink glitter effect like a mini explosion. Then she said, 'Abra-Ca-Daboid', and a full-size elephant appeared next to the girls without a puff of smoke or anything – it was just there, like it always had been.

'Right, off you go then', said the kindly troll as she busied herself stuffing fluff back into a soft toy anteater.

Pheebs began to climb on – handily there was a little step ladder right next to the elephant 'Are you coming?' she blurted down to her sister. 'Um, okay', Rosie replied, slowly clambering up into position.

The elephant introduced herself as Ellie. She spoke with a slow, deep, kind voice. 'All aboard, little ones – let's take a tour'. What happened next surprised them both. Each of the creature's feet sprouted four inline wheels just like roller blades, and off she skated as gracefully as ice skater with long, eloquent strides.

Ellie began to recite her guided tour. 'If you look to the left, you will notice the Museum of National Naughtiness. That is where we celebrate all the naughty but nice things that happen in the city. Over on your right-hand side, you can see the smallest tower behind our city walls. In fact, you probably can't see it without a magnifying glass, but trust me, it's there.

'Excuse me', asked Rosie. 'Where are we going?'

'Ah, a fine question by a fine person', answered Ellie. 'We are rather hoping you are here to rescue the king, and what I'm doing now is taking you on a pretend tour so that the gnomes don't suspect anything. At the right moment, I'll drop you off at court, and you can get our king back!'

Both girls looked concerned. Elle continued, 'Those annoying little sock-stealing gnomes, for some reason, they think socks are people of importance:

Dukes, Lords, Ladies, Counts, Duchesses – you get the idea. They have taken over our King's court and replaced his council members with socks of different sizes.

'What does size matter?'

'Never mind that', said Ellie. 'We all know that you are here to help. All the market traders have been preparing and waiting for you. This is a carefully thought-out plan. I'm going to skate around the stalls and shops a bit, and then at the prime moment, buck you off into a door. 'I don't want to be bucked off', said Pheebs, panicking. 'Fear not, it's all for show, we have a crash mat set up in the doorway – just play along, they are watching'.

The girls tepidly glanced up and occasionally saw a little, colourful gnome hat poking over the top of the battlements.

'Now, ladies, coming up to your left, you will notice a giant cow's backside. This is one of our most treasured works of art. The bottom, known locally as "rumpy" was built over the course of 13 years by acclaimed artist and keeper of the city key, Spetius the Floppy Chicken.

Spetius has worked on many famous artistic pieces, including the great hedgehog butt and the world-famous Bottom Attack – a tribute to the Battle of the Bottoms in 17BS'.

'17BS?' questioned Pheebs.

'Yes, BS means 'Before Smidge' – he's been ruling the fair city for a thousand rotations'.

'Battle of the Bottoms? That sounds stupid', added Rosie.

'Oh yes, quite stupid', said Ellie. 'Lots of creatures fighting for three different armies who previously agreed that the bottom was mightier than the sword. In some ways, it was a good way to fight, as no one ever got particularly hurt. We learned all about it in history class at school.

All of the soldiers would line up opposite each other – well, due to there being three armies, it was more of a triangle arrangement.

One referee would stand in the middle and shout, 'BEGIN!' – then the soldiers would pull their pants down and charge backwards, sticking their bottoms out. Apparently, it was very funny because most of the soldiers lost their balance and fell over.

Only a few ever met in the centre of the battlefield, and because they were running backwards, they mostly missed each other and kept running.

Rumour has it that one particularly odd soldier is still charging around bottom first to this day.

Rosie wondered to herself why this war was ever fought and how it ended up being settled, but thought better than to ask, so decided to shrug at Pheebs, who was happily smirking away at the mental image in her mind.

They continued to trot past all sorts of bright, bold wonders. As they drew level with a handful of jugglers, Ellie described how the ancient jugglers of old had lost their juggling balls centuries ago and transitioned to juggling with rocks instead, which was very hazardous for the new trainees.

Luckily, over 100 new businesses had sprouted from the opportunity to manufacture juggling helmets. The three jugglers and two apprentices were spoilt for choice in head protection.

But tragically, this caused a mini-recession in the juggling trade, which had knock-on effects on the metal, plastic, and paint industries, causing something boring called hyperinflation. 'Long story short', said Ellie, 'they ended up juggling with tennis balls instead'.

The three of them came to a sudden halt. 'Okay, children, we are here. Can you see that curtain over there?' Ellie raised a leg so that her front right roller-hoof was pointing at a tower with a red curtain concealing an opening behind. There were two guards standing in front, they were most definitely frogs with tiny little helmets and sausages instead of spears. They looked taller than the average grown-up human.

'In about ten seconds from now', Ellie was counting in her head. My friends will cause a distraction. When the guards hop away, I'll throw you both into that curtain, understand?'

'Wait', protested Rosie. 'What are we supposed to do when we get th...' Before she could finish her question, there was a huge and very offensive-sounding passing of wind (fart if you want to be rude).

A few of the market traders had thrown their goods all over the ground and were angrily lining up in opposing ranks, beginning to roll up their tunics and turning back-to-back. One of the bystanders shouted, 'BUTT FIGHT!' which caught the attention of the frog guards, who hopped into action towards the commotion, their sausages flopping around as they went.

'Go, go, go!' belted Ellie, and as she artistically pirouetted on her wheels so that her front legs raised and she spun rump-first towards the door, sliding the girls down her back and onto the cushioned mat within the doorway.

Courtside

Pheebs led the way, brushed off the wooden shards, and swished through the curtain with a dramatic performance, just like their older cousin during family plays. They continued down several stone-clad corridors, winding staircases, and through very grand-looking archways.

None of the medieval-themed interiors offered much charm except for one painting they passed on the wall, it seemed to depict a human-looking king being crowned as a little boy.

He was surrounded by pixies hovering, fussing with his hair and make-up. They all wore old-fashioned robes decorated with gemstones and looked on fondly at the young king. In return, he looked like he was laughing and joking with those nearest to him, he was both dashing and handsome.

Rosie thought to herself that it looked like a happy, peaceful occasion and rather hoped it was King Smidge. Suddenly, her emotions bolted – if it was the King, what if she got embarrassed? He was lovely to look at, in the traditional dark hair blue eyes sort of way, the last thing she needed during a rescue was to get distracted.

Several dimly lit corridors later, they emerged onto a huge balcony overlooking the throne room. The entire chamber was surrounded by a golden mural splitting the walls from the ceiling. The mural seemed to show all the creatures of the Hubbub. There were dogs, dolphins, crabs, fairies, trolls, anteaters, genies, goblins, and lots of other odd creatures you've never even heard of.

The girls physically turned in circles, trying to take in the entire work of art. Sometimes, it showed creatures talking and looking very serious. Then it showed tears, laughter, even death! It was overwhelmingly beautiful and hypnotic to look at.

'You know what this is, don't you, Pheebs? – this shows the equi.. equi.. Oh, I don't know how to say it. That word for balance that Willow was talking about'.

'Does it?' said Pheebs, transfixed on a goblin pouring a bucket of liquid over a seahorse sunbathing on a sausage.

'Yes, look. You see that squid there? He's happily talking to the underwater hedgehog'.

'It's not an underwater hedgehog, it's a normal hedgehog wearing a snorkel'.

'And there – right below them, those two fish are arguing over that armchair, and the pixies swimming around in those air bubbles, well, they are crying'.

'But not those ones', added Pheebs, looking at another two. 'They're laughing'. She was referring to another pair of pixies playing hide and seek on a giraffe's head.

'Exactly', said Rosie. 'This is the balance of the Hubbub, it's what Willow was trying to explain'.

Unexpectedly, as if by a magical, invisible force, all four of the sisters' eyes locked onto a single point of the display. It showed a giant set of ancient measuring scales perfectly balanced with hundreds of Hubbub creatures in each of the cups on the two sides – they were, of course, doing a bit of everything, from laughing on pogo sticks to vomiting off motorway bridges, back-slapping while upside down water-skiing, and holding hands jumping into a passing plane.

'It's showing balance', whispered Pheebs, spellbound by the image. 'Look, the scales are perfectly level with one another'. She slowly lifted her head, her gaze rising above the giant scales, revealing a huge pair of human hands, palms facing up with the four fingers coming to a point and touching the thumbs like a sock puppet shape.

Try it if you like? You have to close your fingers against the thumb to make a mouth opening and closing, well, imagine doing that and then turning your hands upside down. Then spread out your arms like an offering of peace. That's what was at the top of the mural. It gave the impression that these hands oversaw the whole picture.

'You don't think those hands are the snappies, do you, Rosie?' She shifted her view onto Rosie, who was busy scanning back around like she was trying to understand every detail. 'I doubt it, but stranger things have happened in this place'.

Pheebs was about to point out that she was certain they were the snappies when suddenly, a loud commotion stirred below them. The noise of shuffling feet on wooden floors was only interrupted when a trumpet sounded a short fanfare.

'Lords and Ladies of court, please rise for your king'.

Rosie and Pheebs broke their gaze from the mural and took a step towards the edge of the balcony, staring down into the royal chamber. Flanked by golden statues of past kings and queens, they watched as King Smidge paraded into the chamber with several sock-stealing gnomes behind him.

'Please sit', he announced as he relaxed into an ornate throne, which looked to be made from a single, huge red gemstone. 'I call the court to order', he continued, glancing over at the gnomes as if to check he was saying the right thing.

Rosie thought the king looked tormented, deeply sad, and void of life, it was clear he was being held captive, just as the Dino Rex had explained. She peered further down into the chamber, sure enough, the king was surrounded by socks with crudely drawn faces. Some were sitting on mini sock-sized chairs, some were being dangled by those idiot gnomes, and silly head had 3 or 4 balanced over his head spikes.

'First order of the day', shouted one of the gnomes (Pheebs recognised it to be Dooey). Dooey was pretending to speak through a grey, woolen sock, the type you might wear skiing.

'I, Lady Fromage, would like to address the proposal for donkey drainage in the lower western sector of the city. We will not abide by donkeys doing their business (and by that, I mean wees and poos) in the streets! The plans for the sub-terranean donkey-doo canal have now been submitted to the appropriate..'.

'I object', shouted a green-pant-wearing gnome. 'We in the east support the right for donkeys to wee and poop wherever they should choose – all in favour?' A collective 'aye' was echoed by all gnome-controlled socks, apart from Dooey, whose sock followed up with a solemn-sounding 'nay!'

After a few seconds of silent reflection, the awkward quiet was broken by tiny footsteps running from out of sight underneath the balcony. Booey sprung into sight and sprinted up to King Smidge, sharply kicking him in the shins. 'Pay attention, sire!' he shouted.

The startled king, who had been falling asleep, raised his head from his hands and pronounced that the motion had been rejected and donkeys could continue to do their business as normal.

'How can we get down there to rescue him?' whispered Pheebs, leaning back behind the balcony parapet. 'I think it's too dangerous', Rosie countered. 'They might capture us too!' What happened next would go down in Pheebs's life as her single bravest moment, which is odd given that all the bravery required was actually from Rosie, Pheebs only really had the idea.

'You see that big flag, curtain thing', Pheebs said eagerly, 'when I give the word, climb down it, grab Smidge, and run for the back door, I'll meet you in the streets'. Before Rosie had a chance to protest the ridiculous idea, Pheebs sprang to her feet and shouted over the edge, 'Oi! Stupid Gnomes, up here!'

They all turned dramatically, like they had seen a ghost. Silly head did a little jump at the same time, and a sock fell off his head. 'Release the king!' she bellowed. 'This is your one and only chance'.

Looey, the gnome closest to the king dropped his yellow elephant sock, which hit the throne on the way down, knocking off one of the googly, stuck-on eyes. 'Get her', he shouted, and all the other gnomes started to charge out back under the balcony towards the stairs. 'NOW!' screamed Pheebs, sprinting away to beat the gnomes to the bottom.

Rosie froze in fear, she was alone. It was quiet, and there was only one thing she could do now thanks to Pheebs. She edged close to where the huge drape hung from the ceiling high above to the floor down below.

She was still crouched so that the king and Looey didn't spot her. Not that the king would notice her – he'd nodded off.

She carefully reached up to grab the material, the curtain-like material felt silky and smooth in her hands. It jostled as she wrestled for a better grip, desperately hoping the remaining gnome wouldn't notice.

The king half opened one eye, scanning the chamber around him. He was not asleep, as it happened, but aware something interesting was happening. Suddenly, his demi-eye was drawn to movement above, where he saw two little hands poking over the top of the balcony, not so subtly trying to grip his favourite purple banner.

The head of a young human girl followed, along with the rest of her body, clumsily climbing over the edge and onto the banner.

He had to act fast! 'Excuse me, gnome', he said politely. 'Have you any room at court for an ambitious lord and lady who have represented my interests for many years?'

'Perhaps – how wealthy are they? How many castles do they own?'

'Oh, many', the king continued. 'If you untie the ropes around my hands, I can show you them'. 'Hmmm', said the gnome.

'Nice try, you'll not fool me that easily'.
'But look', said Smidge as he rolled up his right trouser leg with his left boot, revealing a very plain brown sock. The gnome was taken aback with shock.

'You naughty king! How long have you been keeping this a secret?' 'Well, I have been wearing socks ever since you captured me, if that's what you mean'.

Looey began to kneel facing the king's feet and with his back to Rosie, who was now halfway down the banner and thrashing about like a fly caught in a spider web. It was a miracle that the gnome hadn't spotted her yet.

'My dear Lord and Lady', said Looey, who started to untie the king's boots, 'I do apologise for this inconvenience, had we realised, we would have liberated you both long ago'.

'Such a weirdo', Smidge whispered under his breath. 'Once released from your prison, I shall see to it that you are given a seat at the highest table. Indeed, I hereby name you Lord Balderdash and Lady Plankton, keepers of the king's guard'.

Meanwhile, on the far side of the room, Rosie's descent wasn't going well. Her hands were tired from gripping the silk, and she could barely hold herself up. She was still too high to drop and had to decide on her next move. She felt like the whole banner was sagging with her weight as the fear of falling rose higher in her mind.

She began to tremble and was on the verge of losing control. With each passing second, the terror was at risk of overwhelming her, she tried desperately to slow her breathing, to focus and reset.

Remembering a phrase she once heard her uncle say from his favourite novel, she forced herself to speak out loud, 'Fear is the... Fear is the... Fear is... the something killer... wait... fear is the mind killer!' For no obvious reason other than saying it, she managed to snap out of her anxious state just long enough to come up with a plan.

Holding on for dear life, she started to swing left to right and back again until she could kick herself off the side of the wall with momentum. After several strong swings, she tugged down hard when at her furthest swing, causing the opposite top of the banner to start ripping from the giant rail.

Two swings and two tugs later, the banner tore and dropped, as did she. Immediately, in mid-air, she crawled up the falling material, pushing it below her so that all the soft fabric was forced underneath, creating a nice cushion to land on. It was all over in an instant and was beautifully silent. She hopped up from the pile with newfound confidence and began to run towards Smidge and the kneeling gnome.

The rescue

Pheebs reached the bottom of the stairway just in time to see a flash of underwear colour as the gnomes rounded the corner. They were only a few metres away, maybe 10 at most, and still on the hunt. She could hear their little squeaks and noises as they came. 'This is for the earl of earwax!' said one. 'We'll get her good this time,' screamed another.

Her choice was simple: either try to hide somewhere, or head out to the busy street and lose them in the hustle and bustle. She was an expert at hide and seek back home, but she couldn't see a single nook or cranny to get behind right now.

She looked harder, whispering to herself 'there must be somewhere, a rug to get under, an old chest to hop in', there was nothing to be seen.

She flicked her head back and forth, panicking, trying to decide which option would help her get back to Rosie quicker, which would be the safest? How much time did she have left? About 5 metres at most. Uh oh, that was half her time already.

'Okay, calm down,' she told herself. 'Even if I could find somewhere to hide, that'd be scary. They would no doubt prowl about the place slowly looking, and ready to pounce,' just like playing with her dad. 'That was nerve-racking enough,' she thought. Suddenly she felt homesick and missed her parents.

The simple things like playing hide and seek made her feel safe. How she longed to be back at home, squished into her sister's wash basket, trying to keep still and silent. 'uh-oh, time's up!' She could feel them approaching without having to look. Time to run, she thought. She shifted her body, ready to sprint: 3, 2, 1 – 'WAIT! You there, surrender or else!'

'Dang it,' Pheebs mouthed. Why had she taken so long? All the gnomes stood an arm's reach away and were spreading out, surrounding her.

'You humans think you're so smart – well, this time we have you trapped. Give us your other sock immediately!' commanded all of the gnomes together.

Back in the main chamber, Rosie had locked eyes with King Smidge. She was sneaking up to them both with Looey still wrestling to relieve Smidge of his sock. The king was bending his toes over, trying to make the procedure as tricky as possible.

Rosie tip-toed the final few steps and shrugged her shoulders, unsure of what to do. She considered trying to push the little fellow, but given his size, that seemed a little cruel. Her mind wandered to the next idea – she could talk to him. 'I'm sure he's reasonable sometimes, actually perhaps not, not after last time'.

The king could clearly see she was weighing up her options but could also feel the sock beginning to become untangled from his cramped toes.

'Fear not, brave aristocrats, your time of torment is almost over,' Looey tugged hard with a high-pitched 'heaveeee' and managed to get the first sock off, tumbling backward for a few steps.

Tucking the sock in his back pocket, he went back for the second. Smidge mouthed something to Rosie who had somehow managed to sidestep out of the gnome's path as he shot back.

'cratchhh dawn bhnd ham'.

'What?' Rosie whispered back.

'CRATCH DAWN BHND HAM,'

Smidge repeated, exaggerating his mouth movements.

'I don't understand,' mouthed Rosie, holding her hands out in confusion.

Smidge waited a few more seconds until he could squish his toes up no more. 'Crouch down behind him, now!' The hammer dropped (that means she understood!). Rosie fell onto all fours, making a little bridge directly behind the gnome who yanked off the sock that same second.

The momentum pulled him back again, hitting Rosie's trap perfectly. He hit the floor with a thump, dropping the sock and looking up in horror at his assailant as he rolled over backwards, his little legs ended up over his head so that his pink-pant-wearing butt was pointing at the sky.

Rosie wasted no time. She skipped up to the king, 'let's go,' she shouted excitedly. 'Excellent work,' replied the handsome king, 'but first...' He stalked up to the gnome who was still struggling to stand upright and kicked him so hard that he rolled all the way down the main chamber.

'That was a bit mean,' Rosie said. 'Don't worry, they love rolling, and I'm pretty sure they don't feel pain like us – let's go'. Smidge grabbed Rosie's hand. She blushed, and they darted off through a door to the right of the throne. 'We need to find my sister, she's distracting all the other gnomes,' Rosie managed to blurt out on the move.

Meanwhile...

'You don't want this sock,' Pheebs proudly declared, 'I trod in dog poop earlier'. A kind of cute little gnome took a few steps closer and began to crouch a little towards her feet. 'What's your name then?' asked Pheebs, keeping dead still. 'Vooey,' came the baby-like answer. She wore sky-blue pants with an orange hat.

'You're a little cutey, aren't you?' Vooey slowly leant over just a few inches from the sock. 'Yep yep yep, I'm the cute one of the bunch. Do you want to see my adorable pose?' The little gnome straightened herself and clasped her hands together under her chin, squishing her neck up to strike a position like a puppy begging for food. Her big blue, bright eyes turned cartoon-like, and she began to giggle in glee.

'Hey, stop that!' came the order from the other gnomes. 'Stay on mission and retrieve that sock'. Vooey seemed to snap out of it and darted down, her hand stretched out for the little cotton number. 'HOLD!' shouted the king as Smidge and Rosie rounded a dimly lit corridor into view.

Silly Head did not hesitate, he sprinted up the grand staircase behind, assumed the roly-poly position with his head tucked round under his legs, squatting into a ball. 'Kablahhh,' he shouted but didn't move. 'Kablahhhhhhh,' he repeated, which reminded the other gnomes that he could do with a push. So Booey, and Fooey joined him upstairs, grabbed him by his upturned legs and rocked him back and forth until they had enough momentum to fire him off toward the king and Rosie.

Silly Head picked up speed immediately, perhaps the stairs were steeper than they looked, or perhaps he had a hidden talent for acceleration. Who knows? But either way, Smidge and Rosie had plenty of time to step slightly out of the way and watch him fire in between them both. 'nugnugnugnugnugnugnug,' he repeated as he rolled off into the distance with no suggestion of slowing down.

'Anyway...' sighed Smidge. 'Release her at once. I command
you as king of the...'

'No, it's okay,' interrupted Pheebs. 'I quite like this little one.
Here you go,' she said politely as she removed her right sock
and offered it up to Vooey. Vooey flinched, almost dropping
the sock as the sound of an enormous crash echoed up the
corridor from the direction of Silly Head.

The noise reminded Rosie of bowling when the ball strikes the pins, and you have to do that awkward little walk back to the bench while everyone watches. She almost missed being awkward, another reminder that they must get back to the real world soon.

'Success,' pronounced Vooey with glee beaming on her face. She mouthed 'thank you' to Pheebs and trotted back to the others, handing the sock over to Booey, who looked pleased to be involved. Meanwhile, Looey had caught up and joined his companions.

'Good Grief!' he declared. 'Is that the Lady of Wiltshire?' Looey snatched Pheebs' tiny sock from Vooey. 'It is... it is... I cannot believe it. After all these years, you've been found – and alive too!'

Both the girls and Smidge glanced at each other as if to say 'Not again...' but Rosie had an idea.

'Oh yes, that's the Lady of Wiltshire. We have been looking after her for a while now. You better take her back to Wiltshire Castle. She's been longing to go back and see her sock family'.

Pheebs piped up, 'Eh? That makes no sense.

'Shhh,' replied Smidge and Rosie at the same time. Pheebs understood. 'Quickly, no time to lose,' said Smidge. 'She must be returned to her rightful seat. The work here in my kingdom can wait for you to return. I can run things for a day or two'.

All of the gnomes huddled together like a sports team trying to hide their half-time talk. This went on for several minutes until Booey raised his head to speak and drew a great breath. Before he could say a word, Vooey shoved his head back into the huddle and raised his own head, knocking his hat off in the process.

'We have decided the good Lady must be returned home. We will leave immediately! 'They all formed a little line with Booey forced to the back and marched off down the same tunnel that Silly Head had shot off into.

As they left Pheebs silently snuck up behind Booey and snatched both her and Rosie's missing socks from his back pocket.

The Reward

An hour or so had passed since the gnomes had moved on. The girls found themselves sitting in front of a roaring fire, green flames bellowing out as they lounged on huge, comfy armchairs next to King Smidge.

They were all sipping tea. In fact, the two sisters had politely asked for hot chocolate when offered a cup of tea, and it was the tastiest either of them had ever tried. Complete with whipped cream and marshmallows, yet for some reason, it was served in an ice cream cone instead of a mug.

Smidge addressed them both in a soft, kingly voice. 'So then, thanks are in order. I'm not sure I would have ever escaped without you. I can only assume I was drugged with sleepy medicine the whole time, it all felt a bit like a dream, you see'.

'Yes, I do see', replied Rosie. 'I thought this was all a dream for a long time before I realised the truth: we are stuck here'.

'Stuck here? Nonsense. Where exactly are you from?'

'We are from England, and we live near the beach', said Pheebs. 'We followed a glowing light in the sea and ended up here in the Hubbub'.

'I see'. Smidge looked thoughtful, stroking his chin. Rosie thought about how angular the shape of his face looked. 'You know, I come from England too. At least I think I do. Time mostly stands still down here, so I can't remember very well, but I think I was from a place called Thatchnet – no wait, Thanet, yes, that's the one. Thanet was somewhere near the bottom of the country, but one day I swam out to sea and got pulled down here, just like you, must have been, oh I don't know… a thousand years ago'.

In actual fact, Smidge (formerly Barry Smith) had left Margate Beach only 136 years ago, but time was indeed odd in the Hubbub.

'Don't you want to go home?' Rosie questioned.

'Absolutely not – I love living here. No two days are the same. Sometimes, a mermaid with a mini sausage monster on her back takes your dinner order, and other days, when volunteering in the shelter, the pixie godmothers turn up and create magic mansions for all the homeless to live in. It's a wonderful place.

Pheebs couldn't help herself. 'Also, he's a king! So, there's that'.

'Not really', said Smidge. 'Bit of a pain being a king, to tell you the truth. If it's not sock gnomes invading, it's toilet goblins attacking parliament or monkey-headed worms digging up all the marshmallows. Rules are rules, though. I was made king by winning the cheese-chopping competition, so what can you do? Only 7 rotations left.

'Pheebs and I were wondering if we might be allowed tickets to something called a snappy show. Apparently, it might be our way back home'.

'The snappy show? Of course, it's tonight, isn't it? I'd forgotten all about it. Here, you can have my two tickets. I take no joy in watching those two since they fell out and plunged this whole place into a state of non-balance.

'Ahh, the whole no equilibrium thing?' asked Pheebs, who looked pleased with herself for remembering the word.

'Yes, indeed I do', replied Smidge. 'Sorry, been a bit out of it recently. Not sure if I was in the mood when the change happened or if it was a knock-on effect from all the medicine those gnomes were feeding me. Either way, take my tickets, go and enjoy yourselves'.

'Or you know… I could just show you the way out?'

As King Smidge released the final 't' in this sentence, a chill ran through the room, almost putting out the fire and leaving a very uneasy feeling for all three of them.

'That was odd', said the king. 'But seriously, the way out is just through that door'.

He pointed to a very plain-looking wooden door with a single black iron knocker. 'Come on', he said and stood up, gesturing for the girls to follow him. Smidge opened the door with a slow, ominous creak and stepped through.

Rosie and Pheebs followed him into a giant cage the size of a Football pitch There was a huge crowd surrounding them on all sides, seats were full of interesting Hubbub creatures, and a deafening roar went up when the three of them stepped through.

On the other side of the cage stood a weird monster. It was as tall as the height of the cage, roughly a five-story house. It was pink, weird, and wobbly – I say wobbly as that's simply the easiest way to describe the creature. Imagine a giant sausage made out of jelly, with limp dangling arms and tiny, short little legs.

His face was made up of two crosses for eyes and a straight line for a mouth, as if drawn on with a pencil. In his left hand was a tiny little sword (about the length of Rosie), and in his right was a round shield.

'Only trouble is', said King Smidge, 'you must beat this chap in hand-to-hand combat to get out. That's why I've never bothered trying. This crowd of onlookers seems to be here day and night too. Sometimes I pop through the door at 4 am, and the monster and all the crowd are still here. Waiting, just in case.

Pheebs and Rosie considered their options. 'Well, it does look pretty big and scary', Rosie said, she took half a step back towards the exit.

'C'mon, we can take him', Pheebs suggested, with a foot stomp.

There was silence for a few seconds as the girls locked eyes and considered their options. Before either spoke next or questioned how stupid this was, Smidge interjected:

'So now you've seen the alternative, I assume you'll be wanting those tickets?'

'Yes, please', Rosie answered, knowing full well what her silly sister would probably be thinking. 'That seems like a less dangerous option'.

An odd bus

As Rosie and Pheebs left the castle, they noticed the little Dino-Rex still sitting cross-legged, staring up at them exactly where they had left him earlier. 'What doing?' he belted out. 'Well', replied Rosie, 'We managed to rescue the king by defeating those stupid gnomes again, and he gave us the tickets we need for the snappy show.

Then we can...' Before Rosie had the chance to continue, Dino rudely interrupted, 'Where's my ticket?' The girls suddenly remembered that the Dino-Rex had asked them to get him a ticket too! Pheebs was the first to talk after a little awkward silence.

'Well, you see, after we rescued the king, he offered us two tickets. As we need to find our way home, we had better use them ourselves. Is there another way you can get a ticket?

We must help the snappies become friends again, you see. That's the only way we can get home'.

'No ticket for Dino?' the little Rex shouted and stood for the first time in a while. 'NO TICKET?' 'Then I ta-tack!' 'Do you mean attack?' asked Rosie innocently. 'YESSS ta-tack!' The Dino charged at the little girls, head down, mini arms behind his back. He bounced off Rosie's leg and fell backwards, with Rosie barely losing her balance.

He jumped back to his feet. 'TA-TACK!' he screamed as he charged again, This time he didn't even make it as far as the kids, he tripped on his own feet and hit the dirt in front of them. Again, he sprang back to his feet. 'TA-TACK!' came the shout.

'Hang on, hang on', said Rosie. 'Look, I'm sure there is something we can do to get you a ticket. Didn't you say the king had a queen and a son? He must have 3 tickets in total. I'm sure if we just go back and ask him, then he'll happily give us a third'.

'It's too late, little childrens. Now I is eating you', he opened his mouth wide, revealing some surprisingly sharp teeth. Before he had the chance to advance on them again, they all heard a deafening, yet somehow quiet noise...'sssssssss'.

'What in the heck?' wondered Pheebs. 'Sssssssss', it came again.

Away to the south (was it the south? No one really knows), they saw a huge snake-like creature, probably the length of 15 buses, slithering along with what looked like hundreds of creatures on its back. The snake had an enormous head, a bit like a king cobra, except it was bright orange.

The slithery body was light green in colour and seemed to move by creating lots of U shapes in its body to create momentum. The way in which it pushed itself along looked far from ideal, for all the passengers were holding on for dear life. Every few yards, a duck-headed yeti or rainbow fairy would fall off or get launched far away as the mammoth snake contracted into another series of U shapes.

'Look! It's the snakey fellow', said the Dino Rex, who didn't see anything unusual in all this. Rosie stared in awe and simply sighed out a long breath, she was certainly becoming fatigued with all the silliness going on. 'Hey!' screamed Pheebs at the snake. 'Where are you going?' The snake turned its head menacingly towards the trio and let out a substantial 'ssssss' before looking away again and creating a series of bends in its body.

This time, a family of otters in knickers went flying off above the clouds as the dad could be heard shouting 'Blimmin heck, not again!'

'What meaning?' said Dino. 'I want to know where they are all heading'. Pheebs said, 'They going to snappy show. Anyway… TA-TACK'. 'No wait, wait', said Pheebs.

They had managed to catch up with the snake bus (as Rosie decided to call it). 'Come on, quick! It's not slowing down', she yelled as she grabbed her little sister and helped her clamber up into a group of ostrich-headed flamingos.

Rosie got herself on without too many problems and looked back to the Dino, who was struggling to keep up. 'I'm tired', he shouted to them. 'Snakey fellow is too fast'. Rosie didn't hesitate, she grabbed the tail of a nearby field mouse.

It wasn't a normal tail, by the way. If the mouse was a normal size (which it was), then the tail was 50 times bigger. 'Excuse me', she said to the mouse, 'Can I borrow this?' Without waiting for a reply, she swung the tail around her head like a lasso and launched it off towards the Dino-Rex.

'Catch it!' screamed Pheebs. The Dino blindly held up his hands as he ran but had no luck, the tail hit him square in the head and knocked him over. Dino groaned as he hit the floor. 'Don't worry', squeaked the mouse, who positioned it's tail to wrap around the Dino-Rex and haul him up to safety.

'What doing? said the Dino as he was delivered in between the girls. 'Right', said Rosie, 'Hang on to something'. She had spotted that the snake's giant U-shaped bends were forming up ahead as it rushed along in a slither. 'Ohh nooo', she heard a pixie shout as she launched skyward, luckily she fluttered back down to her spot peacefully.

'Here we go', screamed Pheebs, lying down and clinging to the snake's body. Rosie and Pheebs exchanged looks when the body beneath them contracted up faster than they expected, like one of those crazy sling-shot rides. 'Weeeee', they both heard behind them. They turned to see the Dino-Rex take off like a bullet, flying up and up. 'Off I go...' they picked up in a distant voice as they left him for dust and sped off.

Some time and many contractions later, the girls found themselves dropped off at a very busy theatre entrance. The snake, who had offloaded all passengers by tilting sideways until everyone had slid off, let out an enormous 'ssssss' and slithered off. Interestingly, it didn't seem to be making U-shapes anymore and seemed much calmer. Rosie wondered if it had been just trying to throw people off for fun.

The two of them walked into the stadium cautiously. It was a little like one of those giant football stadiums you see on the telly. Various creatures in red suits were checking tickets, there were green fairies selling programs, lizards in ice cream vans, and one small frog standing on its head, reciting a poem about fishing.

'This way', Rosie said, grabbing Pheebs by the hand and running towards a set of stairs that said rows A-Z, Levels 1-100. As it turns out, everyone else was also heading this way, except for a group of leprechauns who were muttering about having 10 pints of black stuff before it started.
The girls reached a series of ladders, which, according to the various signs, led them to their seats. 'Considering that Smidge is a king, he doesn't get very good seats', said Pheebs, with her neck cranked up, looking at how high these things seemed to go.

Surrounding the foot of the ladders was a series of round trampolines all buried in the floor so that they sat about 10 feet lower than the ground level. 'Right then, shall we?' said Rosie, bravely gripping the sides of the first ladder.

Before she could start climbing, there was a terrible wail as a very small rabbit with purple, spikey hair shot passed them both, falling from high above. The creature fell straight into the sunken trampolines and seemed to bounce back onto the floor, level with the perfect amount of height so that it landed perfectly. With a huff of failure, the rabbit stomped off.

'Oh my gosh – I'm not so sure about this', said Rosie, releasing her grip from the ladder. 'Oh, it's not so bad when you get used to it' replied a familiar voice.

Show time

The girls looked down beside them, lo and behold, Willow the dog was there. She sat, peering up skywards with the children. 'No really, it's not as bad as it looks if you know the proper technique'.

'What are you doing here?' Rosie asked. 'Oh, I'm just popping in to check you get your quest done – you remember? The whole thing about equilibrium? Making the snappies become friends again? C'mon, it wasn't that long ago we discussed it'.

'All I remember', Rosie replied, 'is you being very serious, then laughing at Phoebe's stupid fart noise'. Both Willow and Pheebs gave out a little chuckle as they remembered how funny it had been.

'Right then', Willow shouted sternly, 'follow exactly what I do and it'll be a breeze'. The small dog moved in front of Rosie at the ladder, positioned herself into a handstand, gripped both sides of the ladder with her hands and feet, and said, 'Basically, it's like an upside-down gravity force.

You can't really walk up the ladder, you have to slide it – but the wrong way round'. She began moving slowly up the rungs by sliding on the sides – she was still upside down.

'You see, the more I release my grip, the faster up I go, just like if I were sliding down'. Suddenly, she shot up to the first level where the second ladder began and jumped off the ledge into the trampoline pit, hopping back up perfectly to ground level.

'You see, girls, it's simple'.

'Oh my gosh!' Pheebs exclaimed. 'I'm not doing that!

Upside-down sliding up ladders is not for me'. Rosie sighed, she certainly shared this opinion but cautiously approached the ladder and went down to the ground.

She positioned her feet on the third rung and awkwardly twisted her body around so that her front was pressed up against the ladder.

She shifted up and up until her head almost lay on the ground with her feet pointing straight up, now tucked around the 5th rung.

'Okay', said Willow. 'That's just about it. Now, when you're ready, put your feet on the ladder sides and very slowly release your hands to gradually let yourself slide. Think of a fireman's pole in the park, it's that but backwards'.

Rosie couldn't quite get the hang of it to start with and let go too quickly. She fired up the ladder and was about six rungs up before she grabbed tight again and came to a stop, now hanging upside down in the air.

'That's the idea!' Willow shouted. 'Keep going up but try to release your grip slower!' Mostly out of desperation, she had a little word with herself. 'You've got this, Rosie', she whispered and sure enough, she did. In little, short, sharp bursts, she jolted herself up until she was slightly above the first platform and collapsed onto it.

Right behind her, a miniature donkey with sunglasses and a backward cap hopped onto the ladder, spun upside down, and flew up, landing on its feet next to Rosie. 'eeee-ooooo-rrrrrr', it blurted as it plodded over to the next ladder and continued up.

'So… young Phoebe, you're next. Would you like me to help you get in position?' Willow asked. Rosie peered down from above, worried both about her sister and the next ladder she herself had to face.

'No way, not happening', said Pheebs, stomping her foot down with the last 'ing'.

'But it's the only way up, you must, for all our sakes. It's your destiny'. Willow replied in desperation. Defiantly, Pheebs tried to climb up the normal way, but she was immediately zapped with a small electric shock. 'yowwwzers', she squeaked and took a step back, shaking her leg around like a mad dance move on fast forward.

'Come on, Pheebs!' came the call down from her big sister. Reluctantly, she managed to get almost upside down, all squished up against the ladder. 'Right', said Willow. '3, 2, 1, let go of your grip'. Pheebs closed her eyes tightly and let go with both hands. Rather than shooting upwards, she simply rolled face-first onto the floor with a thud.

'What the?' she heard herself say, mumbling into the concrete. 'Ohhh never mind', said Willow. 'We haven't got all day'. With amazing strength, she grabbed Pheebs and flung her up a few feet in the air, while at the same time flipped over, then caught her with her left foot.

Now in a handstand position, Willow grabbed the ladder and shot up. Then, from the platform, she grabbed Rosie too, placing her balanced on her right foot with Pheebs still on the left, and continued to zip up five more ladders until they reached their level.

The three of them were balanced on a very thin plank of wood with nothing to hold on to. Willow turned and marched on with determination and a little impatience. 'Come along, girls, your seats are just over here'.

They noticed that running parallel to the planks were various tightropes and some creatures were egging each other on to use them instead of the planks.

One fairy who was bored of waiting for her troll companion simply glided along with a few flaps of her wings to make it look easy.

The troll, however, didn't quite have the same luck. When stepping out, he immediately stumbled, missed the rope altogether, and ended up plummeting all the way back down to the trampoline pit with a distant howl. He bounced back as normal and made his way up the ladders again.

'Why is this place so dangerous?' Rosie called out to Willow up ahead. 'Dangerous? It's perfectly safe. Now hurry up, you have a job to do'.

A seat fit for a dino

Willow paused by two very comfy-looking seats. 'Now then, these two are where you sit. I'll leave you here and be on my way – good luck, and remember we're all depending on you'. The seats were green leather armchairs – very old-fashioned and fancy.

In fact, all the seats around them were slightly different: some were wooden rocking chairs, others were stools, and there was even the odd toilet too, complete with a working flush and toilet roll holders. The rows all around them – above, below, and on both sides – were filling up quickly with all the amazing inhabitants of the Hubbub.

On Rosie's right, a crocodile wearing brown knee-length leather boots, a top hat and sporting a rather striking moustache sat down upon a toadstool. 'How do you do, my good lady?' he proclaimed with a nod of his hat.

Rosie nervously replied, 'Um, I do fine, thank you,' before turning to her sister in shock. Meanwhile, Pheebs was oblivious, scanning here, there, and everywhere to take in the sights.

The stadium was now full, no seats were left unoccupied, except one. A hushed silence seemed to wash over the crowd. 'I wonder why no one is sitting next to me,' Pheebs said, only noticing the croc for the first time, who simply nodded her way with a smile.

In the distance, both girls could hear a familiar noise, growing slightly louder with every passing second. They locked eyes just in time for Rosie to say, 'Oh no,' as the sound began to crescendo. 'Weee,' they heard from above them. Rosie didn't bother looking – she knew what was happening. Pheebs craned her neck up in time to see the Dino-Rex falling with serious speed, head-first toward the seat next to her.

The next second or two felt like a month to Pheebs. 'Wee, it's still coming,' she thought. She glanced over at the vacant seat to her right, in fact, it wasn't really a seat, more of a wooden barrel – the type a dwarf might travel downriver in. It had a lid – a firmly closed lid. She wasted no time, jumping to her feet, grabbing the lid, and flinging it open a micro-second before the Dino landed with a splash, still headfirst.

Inside the barrel, there was a lot of bubbling going on. The liquid – either water or wine, depending on your interpretation – splashed a little over the rim.

'What doing?' said the Dino-Rex as he popped his head out, 'Is tasty stuffs'. 'Hi Dino,' said Pheebs, trying to help him out of the liquid.

'Hellos, little one – it's okay, I is staying here,' he protested. 'What I miss?'

Pheebs was just about to start explaining when, all of a sudden all the lights in the stadium dimmed to pitch darkness. There was a hush that swept over the crowd like a wall of silence had crashed into all the creatures at once, forcing their mouths and other noise-making orifices shut!

Then, fifty or so spotlights burst into life and shone onto every side of the stadium in bright, brilliant light beams. They slowly moved, tracking down through the stands, over each and every tier of seating from the very top, moving slowly until they reached the ground level all at once, creating the illusion of circles of light dotting around the floor.

There was a huge, booming announcement: 'Ladies, gentlemen, fairies, silly sausage heads, animals, pig-nosed hedgehogs, and everything in between. Welcome to... THE SNAPPY SHOW'. An enormous cheer rose all around the children – it was as big a sound as they had ever heard. The announcer followed up with a 'SHHH' to quiet the excited audience.

A drumroll started, initially from drummers in the band, but very soon, thousands of creatures stamping their feet joined in. The Dino-Rex just splashed a lot.

The spotlights moved in circles around the perimeter of the stadium floor, faster and faster as the drumroll became quicker and quicker. They began to draw in closer now to the centre of the floor, where a giant stage was rising up through a hole, as if driven by the noise from all around.

On top of the stage was a small box, which was almost too far away for the girls to clearly see. It looked a little like those Punch and Judy mini-theatre boxes you sometimes see at the seaside.

As the stage reached its full height, the lights suddenly went out again, plunging the stadium into darkness. The girls held their breath in anticipation, wondering what was going to happen next. Suddenly, a single spotlight shone down on the small box, illuminating it – if a pin had been dropped, it would have been heard.

For several moments, nothing happened. Rosie felt a sharp nudge in her side, the well-dressed croc was holding a pair of binoculars up to his eyes and gesturing for Rosie to pick up her pair, which had magically appeared in front of her. She obliged and signaled for Pheebs to do the same.

Breaking and entering

Both girls had a decent view through the binoculars. They were still far away, so it was hard to keep the view steady, it was all rather shaky and a little blurry, but they did manage to see what happened next.

Two human-looking hands raised through the roof of the box which seemed to be the performance area. They were positioned in such a way that the four fingers were stretched out to touch the thumb.

Imagine your hand was in a sock and you were performing a sock puppet show. Go on, do it now. I'll wait.

No really, try it yourself.

Got it? Good. Sock puppets without socks were pretty much what was going on here. Clearly, there was an adult human inside the box performing so that the only thing visible to the audience were the arms and hands.

Unlike a traditional Punch and Judy show, the mini theatre was three hundred and sixty degrees, so the entire stadium could see the action. The roof of the box was either floating or hanging on very thin wire, I guess we'll never know which.

'Wait, is that it?' asked Pheebs. 'Shh, please', said the posh crocodile. 'No, but seriously, there are thousands and thousands of people here, to watch someone do a show with their hands?' Rosie put her hand over Pheebs' chest as if to say 'hang on, let's see what happens'. Sure enough, something did start to happen.

The left-hand snappy began to snap at the right (try that too if you like). It was also nudging left snappy, who was simply facing the other way and seemingly ignoring the right hand. After several minutes of anticipation, you could feel the crowd's disappointment as sighs were let out and some creatures got up to leave.

Rosie looked to her left and noticed the croc had dropped the binoculars and had its head in its hands. 'Oh no no' it said, 'They still aren't talking to each other – what are we to do? Little snappy is still ignoring big snappy'.

'How do you know which is which?'

'Ah well, little snappy does smaller, baby-like snaps, and you see big snappy does bigger, more aggressive snaps.

'Right', said Rosie. She was well over the realisation that this whole Hubbub place is beyond silly.

'Come on then', Pheebs piped up. 'We need to go and talk to the person in control and sort this mess out'. The croc looked confused. 'Oh, he won't talk to you, although he is your species I suppose. He only talks via big and little snappy, never said a word I heard'.
        'That's why we're here', continued Rosie. The equilibrium of the Hubbub is balanced by those two sna...hands. We need to get them to be friends again'.

'Well, best of luck, little girls. You'll need it'. With that, he abruptly walked off like he hadn't believed a word they had said.

'Dino help', came the sound from next to Pheebs.

'I is taking you down to see snappies'.

And he jumped out of the barrel, splashing both girls in the process. Yep, definitely wine thought Pheebs as she wiped her mouth, thinking how disgusting it tasted. 'Following me?' The Dino-Rex walked along their row, nudging past many creatures who looked a bit depressed with the whole affair.
        Eventually, they reached the top of a humungous red slide. It ran from the very top of the stadium down to the floor, it was a vertical drop for at least the first 20 metres before gradually curving out to a flat surface towards the bottom.

'I hadn't noticed this before', Rosie said, 'it's massive. I don't know how we missed it'.

'Silly billy – big slidy thing always here. Off we go, weeee' the mini dinosaur didn't hesitate as he leapt head-first into the drop. He was caught perfectly by the slide's transition into flat but didn't seem to slow down much, he flew off the end of the slide, taking out a family of mini elephants being ridden by baby bunnies.

'Shall we go together? Pheebs suggested. 'Maybe we can slow each other down as we hit the end'. Rosie agreed, and they stood hand in hand at the top. Both took a deep breath.

Can you imagine seeing a slide run from the top of Wembley Stadium to the pitch? Well, this was bigger. '3, 2, 1, go!' Rosie shouted as they sprang down into freefall. The speed was unreal.

They felt the skin on their faces pulling back against their skulls as they dropped. The wind chill was extreme, a tsunami of cold air flying over them, it felt like it was flowing directly through their bodies, freezing them to the core.

Eventually, the slide caught them with a very smooth feeling as they felt their weight picked up by the surface and were no longer falling. Pheebs managed to get out a noise 'It's too fast... we're going to crash'. There definitely wasn't enough runoff at the end of the slide.

Whoever designed it clearly intended for the riders to go flying off the end. As the girls sped towards the floor, they noticed that Willow was casually walking past the slide's end. She abruptly stopped and opened up a huge rainbow umbrella directly towards the sisters.

'Hold on', Rosie yelled as they hit the material. They were astounded as they slowly came to a halt, the umbrella cushioning their impact without any danger at all.

Willow quickly shook them out as if she were flicking off water before putting away the umbrella. 'Quickly, girls, now is your chance. Do what you need to do'. Rosie got to her feet, still slightly shaking. 'But what do we need to do?' Willow just smirked and walked off into the crowd of creatures, leaving the stadium.

They now stood at the edge of the stage, itself in the very centre of the floor. Tepidly they strolled toward the middle, where the strange little performance was still taking place. Dino was already there, banging on the side of the structure with his front mini T-rex arms. 'EXCUSING ME', he bellowed. 'Excusing me, snappies'.

Neither of the hands pretending to be puppets, or indeed their owner, responded. One snappy simply continued to 'snap' at the other, who still wasn't taking any notice. As the Dino-Rex kept banging, the girls finally reached the box. 'Ok, Pheebs, let's slowly creep in and see if we can speak with whoever is doing the show'. Pheebs was having none of it. She stomped her foot against the ground and marched around the box, expecting to see a curtain, or an entrance of some sort. There wasn't one.

Suddenly, some of the dirt below their feet started to shift. The ground looked like it was giving way and forming a little circle right next to Dino. A few seconds later, a little soil sprayed up into the air and two eyes on stalks popped up from under the earth.

'I knew it!' Rosie let out. 'I knew you had eyelashes when I saw you on the beach at home'. The crab popped out of the ground completely.

'Hello again, lovely day for it'.

'Lovely day for what?' asked Pheebs, walking back around.

'Lovely day for tunnelling, of course. We crabs love to tunnel and skydive. It's what we're known for. I noticed you were trying to get into the snappy show. That's jolly brave of you – no one's ever seen the person in charge of the snappies. Some say it's a demon of some sort, others say a witch. I reckon it's probably a fruit fly, but who knows?'

'It's definitely not a fruit fly, is it?' replied Pheebs.

Before the crab could reply, Rosie interjected. 'Can you please help us to get in?'

'I suppose I could tunnel you through, but I'm not going in there'. Without any hesitation, the crab charged at the box. A split second before she hit the wood, her claws started spinning like helicopter blades and chopped, splintering the wood in no time, creating a small hole big enough for the girls to crawl through.

'There you are, in you pop! Let me know how it goes'. Within a second or two, the crab had dug directly down and away.

Equilibrium

'Ah, hello, girls. You took your time, I was expecting you to knock'.

'Hello', replied Rosie. 'Actually, the dinosaur was knocking rather aggressively'.

'Oh, I never answer when he bangs. I was expecting YOU to knock, like all the others have done, but the crab route? Well, that's a new one for me. I suppose you want to make these two guys friends again, do you?'

Rosie and Pheebs stepped into the box. They saw an older gentleman, perhaps in his sixties, wearing a cardigan, a shirt, and grey slippers.

He was sitting on a blue armchair poking his arms up above him through to the performance area. Both of the children were a little confused and didn't speak up for a second. Eventually, the man broke the silence.

'So, what is it you're here to do?' he spoke as if he had muttered this phrase before.

Pheebs tried first. 'Look, if you're just a normal person pretending your hands are puppets or snappies', she said this with a sarcastic look, 'Or whatever you call them. Just pretend they are friends again, and everyone here can be happy or sad or however they left off, and we can go home'.

'Interesting', he pondered. 'Still different'. The man drew his hands inside the box, the one that was snapping stopped, and they both appeared to face him. 'Well? What do you two think?' he said to his hands. 'Would you just like to be friends again and sort this whole mess out? You go first, little snappy'.

His left hand moved next to the right and started snuggling against the other, knuckles first, a bit like a cat who affectionately rubs its head on humans. Big snappy was pointing in the other direction, not paying attention until it appeared to have enough, opened up, and had one giant snap on little snappy.

They then thrashed around for at least thirty seconds, with the right hand locking into the left and not letting go. This is what the man said during this whole affair.
'Ahh, look, little snappy wants to make up. Come on, big snappy, be nice. Oh, look, he's turning. Wait, no! No, don't do it! Oh my... BIG SNAPPY! Let him go at once. Stop it, you used to be so close. Please stop.

Right, if you don't let go right away, I'll never bring you to perform again'.

During this strange speech, he was also making struggling noises himself, as if the two hands weren't controlled by him at all and were bashing him about as they fought. He even rose to his feet at one point as the momentum of the fight seemed stronger than him.

Rosie and Pheebs just watched, slightly embarrassed for the poor man. 'Right, this is stupid', Rosie lurched forward, grabbing both of the man's forearms and with an effort managed to pry open his arms and release Little snappy from Big snappy's grip. The left hand went limp as if it were injured, now hanging in Rosie's grip, all the while still in a sock puppet shape.

Pheebs spoke: 'How do we make them friends again? Why don't you just tell us?'

The older man glanced over at her. 'It's not as simple as that. While it might look like I'm controlling these little fellas, I can assure you that I'm not. It all started when I was a child, firstly big snappy appeared one day and started snapping me at dinner with my parents. Soon after, little snappy popped up, and they became best friends.

They did everything together, from dancing to clapping until one day not so long ago, little snappy took a snap at the big one while aiming for a fly. Big snappy wouldn't have it and snapped him back... only harder. Little snappy was out of it for days, a bit like it is now, lifeless'.

The man waved little snappy around who was still limp from the savage snap.

'So there is nothing we can do?' asked Rosie.

'Oh yes, there is something you can do. All I said was it's not that simple. Let me tell you what I told the others'.

'Wait. Why does everyone keep talking about others?' asked Pheebs.

'Oh, that? We're living in some sort of looping timeline, multiple dimensions, parallel universes or the like. Try not to think about it too much, otherwise, it sends you a bit doolally'.

It was at that precise moment that Pheebs had a light bulb go off in her head. Not literally, of course, or her brain would probably melt. It's what writers like to call a metaphor, but I guess you know that already. Anyway, she stamped her right foot into the ground.

'I know!' she said. 'Just tell us what the others have done wrong so we know what not to do'.

'Also - what happens to all the other versions of us? Where do they go?'

'Well, I ask them the riddle, and they get the answer wrong, and then they get captured by the Bonk monster. I never see them after that'.

Rosie leaned over and whispered into her sister's ear. 'Let's not ask about the Bonk monster. Keep going, I think you're on to something'.

'Ah! Right, so there's a riddle, and you know the answer?'

'Oh no, only Big snappy knows the answer. He always shakes and never nods, that's how I know it's always the wrong answer'.

The girls were uncertain, the idea of a Bonk monster didn't sound ideal, especially when they were this close to success. Rosie spoke up. 'Can you tell us the riddle, please?'

'Certainly, but beware, you only get one chance:

Here in the Hubbub where balance is key,
Big Snappy and Little Snappy yearn to agree,
High and low, they clash and fight,
To put on a show, they must unite.

In vain, our creatures struggle and weep,
Their equilibrium lost, they cannot sleep,
What will you say, how will you act?
We all need your help, that is a fact.

So, riddle me this, my sweet little miss,
I'm a greeting or feeling to cherish,
What am I? That can be given with love.
Get it right. Or surely, you'll perish.

You can give me or take me with ease,
I can be stolen or blown, as you please,
Share your guess, for all to see,
End our torture, set us free!'

There was an awkward silence as the girls pondered, the old man waited patiently, and the Dino Rex tried to do a backflip but landed on his head.

Pheebs spoke first. 'It's something that can be given with love, and it's a greeting, or a moment to cherish. So like a nice moment, where you can also say hello to someone? Oh – is it a hu…'.

'Quiet', replied Rosie. 'We only have one chance! Anyway, you're wrong, it's obvious, isn't it?' Before waiting for an answer, she marched over to the man, who was smirking with anticipation, and grabbed both the snappies. Rosie forced them together, so all the fingertips were touching.

'Kiss you, idiots! KISS'. The snappies froze for a few moments, still held together, when all of a sudden little snappy started bouncing back and forth like it was giving big snappy lots of kisses. Big snappy reacted, but rather than giving little snappy a big snap, it kissed the other hand back.

Suddenly there was a huge shockwave which exploded from the man's hand and fired out in all directions. It wasn't physical, no one flinched or reacted, but every creature in the Hubbub felt it pass through them, a feeling of change, a feeling of balance.

Equilibrium had been restored.

The man stood up examining his hands who were now playing together, swinging and zooming around in circles like a couple of playful kittens. 'I don't believe it', he said. 'You've done it, look! LOOK AT THEM!'

Rosie and Pheebs could feel the ground beneath them shaking like thousands of people were walking all around them, or perhaps one giant monster. They poked their heads out of the performing hole and to their amazement they saw all the creatures of the Hubbub walking, running, flying, and bouncing back to their seats. '

The show can go on!' the man exclaimed budging past the girls to stick his hands through and start entertaining the stadium which now looked completely full again. 'Well done, girls, well done!' He said pointing his head back.

'You can go now, go back home'.

'Wait', said Rosie, 'that was too easy. How come none of the others got it?'

'Hmm?' The man replied. 'What others? What do you mean?'
'You told us there were other kids like us who tried to help you, they all failed you said'.

'I'm sorry, little girl, I don't remember any of that'.

Pheebs quickly piped up, 'Not just you either, other creatures have told us about all the 'others', what's going on here?'
　　The Dino Rex started to speak, but this time his silly accent was gone, now he spoke like a well-educated gentleman from Surrey.
　　'Oh, it's quite simple really, you see this whole equilibrium change not only affected our state of calm, it must have also exposed our minds to a greater level of consciousness. I for one saw multiple versions of myself at one point, all slightly different mind you but perfectly recognisable as me. I suppose we were able to see glimpses of different realities, different timelines. I don't really understand all this talk of physics and theory myself – but you get the drift.
　　By the way, did you notice how my voice was a little silly before? I think the change happened when I was playing with my young nieces, therefore, my state of mind at the time was overtly silly – all back to normal now, you see? Tally-Ho, time to move on. By the way, thank you for the adventure, most fun I've had in years'.
　　With that, the Dino-Rex bowed his head, tipped his hat, and walked sensibly off to his job as an insurance broker.
With all the commotion and noise of seats filling up outside, they hadn't noticed that the strange little crab had reappeared in the shed.

'Come on then, girls, your work here is done'. She grabbed them both by the hand, jumping up as she did so. Her 8 legs extended down to the ground, and she led them back through the little hole.

'Right then', she said, 'time to take you back – it's a lovely day for tunnelling. Oh, you'll need these'. She handed them both a backpack and jumped through the burrow she'd made earlier in the ground.

The girls, eager to go home, willingly obliged, and after putting on their packs, jumped feet first into the burrow, Rosie first, then Pheebs, who let out a little 'ARGHHH' as she went.

Homeward Bound

'As it turned out, the backpacks were, in fact, parachutes, and the hole they jumped through shot them into the sky. Yep, you read that correctly: a hole in the ground led directly to the clouds.

Free fall is an interesting experience, the emotions tend to jump from pure, unadulterated fear to a feeling of euphoric fun as one becomes used to the speed.

At least that's what we understand from people who do a skydive for the first time. In the case of Rosie and Pheebs, it was quite unexpected that they would find themselves falling face-first, several thousand feet up in the sky, but then again, you'd think they would be used to the surprises by now.

After several seconds of terrifying descent, Pheebs shouted through the wind rushing past her, 'What the heck!' Of course, Rosie couldn't hear a thing other than her own wind noise.

They fell and fell, tumbling head over heels, their legs and arms flailing uncontrollably. Shortly, they caught up with the little crab, who had seemingly spread her multiple legs, making herself as wide as possible.

Rosie noticed this had slowed the crab's fall considerably, so as they plummeted down, she managed to tug at her sister's sleeve and showed Pheebs how to spread her own legs and arms while facing belly down, as if they were laying down on their tummies doing their best starfish impression.

This took considerable effort, all the while the meadows below grew closer by the second. Eventually, they managed to stabilise themselves enough to have very slight communication.

'PALLLL THAA CAARD', Pheebs thought she heard Rosie scream.

'WHAT?' she managed back.

Rosie repeated this phrase several times, but there was no acknowledgement from Pheebs, so she grabbed the cord of her parachute, made a movement to try and show Pheebs what she was doing before pulling the cord and coming to a sudden slowdown and relaxing glide.

Pheebs, on the other hand, continued to plummet. She had no idea how fast: 100mph? 500mph? Who knew? It was actually 150mph and wouldn't get any faster, it was her terminal velocity. Woah, that's a strange phrase, isn't it? It simply means the maximum speed you can fall at.

After what seemed like a lifetime, she understood and felt brave enough to pull her own cord. The slowdown in speed was staggering and felt serene, the relief overwhelmed her, and a tear trickled down her cheek as she too came to a gentle glide.

'Oi – you took your time', came the croaky voice from above her.

'Scared the living daylights out of me, that did'.

Pheebs cranked her neck upwards to reveal her somewhat unusual parachute. What she saw above was as a giant green frog, stretched out flat with its arms and legs connected to the backpack with green rope.

'Oh goodness', Pheebs squeaked, glancing further up above her, she noticed Rosie's parachute was similarly odd. She was using a huge black bat as her chute and, concerningly was nosediving downwards towards her.

Rosie caught up with her sister, swooping in by pulling her ropes controlling the parachute perfectly. 'It's ok Pheebs, these things are really easy to control and quite polite to talk to'.

'Well, polite to you maybe', the bat interrupted, 'but not to Ribet-Boy over there'.

'Blimming heck – not you again!' came the response from Pheebs' frog. 'Look, I've just about had enough of you, why don't you flutter away like the fairy you are, and I'll see you at the bottom!' The frog then tilted its head towards Pheebs. 'That bat is always coming out on the same missions as me, she loves to wind me up, a bit of a bully, to tell you the truth'.

'Why did the crab have a normal parachute?' Rosie interjected.

'Normal, you say? The bat replied. 'That death trap is far from normal, homemade methinks, that's crabs for you I suppose. Right, come on! let's get you down safely'.

'See you at the bottom, greenie!' and the bat began a steep series of circling loops gaining speed down to the ground.

'Oh no, you won't beat me again!' the frog shouted back.

Pheebs' anxiety was rapidly building. 'Please don't go fast, let's just keep it slow and steady'.

'NEVER!' bellowed the frog and proceeded to retract his arms and legs, forming the shape of a frog-ball. The two of them dived, at full speed, quickly zooming past Rosie and her bat, leaving a wake of turbulence behind them as they went.

Rosie panicked as she heard Pheebs' muffled scream as she shot past.

When Rosie finally hit the ground, landing on her feet and running a few steps with the momentum, Pheebs was already down and trying her best to pack the frog-chute back into the backpack.

'I told you we would win', the frog managed to gaggle out before the bag was zipped, and the parachute silenced'.

Wait! What?

The girls found themselves in a strangely familiar place. Looking around, they were in a long, dark tunnel dimly lit with burning torches.

'Oi, Gladdis, look who it is?'

'Blimey, quick, find Gary!' Rosie and Pheebs found themselves back at the entrance of the glow-worm tunnel.

'I say, you there! Follow me!' The crab scuttled away, down the corridor, away from the worms.

'Oi, come back 'ere and get what's comin' to ya', came the tiny cry from behind them as they walked off in haste. Before too long, they stopped, and the crab looked up.

'Ahhh, there we are. You see, back where you arrived'. They stood directly underneath the huge waterfall slide where they had dropped into the Hubbub, the kids' paddling pool at their feet, full of little coloured balls which had been neatly replaced after their splashdown.

Rosie spoke, 'Oh wow, back here. How do we get back up? I really want to go home now'.

'Well, you simply follow me, like I suggested before – although at the time, I was rather hoping you wouldn't – what with saving the Hubbub and all. Off we go then'.

The crab led them no more than five steps around a corner to a green wooden door which simply said the word 'EXIT' along the top.

'Here we are then. If you go through there, you'll find yourselves back in that silly world of yours'.

Pheebs was furious. 'Wait! You mean if we'd followed you when we first arrived, all we had to do was go around this corner and go home? ROSIE! Why did you make us go the other way?'

The crab did a little shrug and reached around behind grabbing some rather funky pink sunglasses and popping them on her eyestalks.

'Oh, come on, Pheebs – it was an adventure, wasn't it?'

Pheebs stomped her leg down in frustration with a humph sound and marched up to the door, opening it wide. The bright light poured in, forcing both girls to look away and cover their eyes. After a few seconds, as Pheebs' eyes became accustomed, she wandered through the doorway without even checking that Rosie was behind her.

'Sorry about her', Rosie apologised to the crab. 'I hope we can meet again one day'. And she turned towards the door and left the Hubbub.

A Tall Tail

'Rosie, Rosie – are you okay?' She slowly opened her eyes, blocking the beaming sun with her hand.

'Wow, that was a hell of a header. Does it hurt?' her dad said, still holding a half-cooked sausage on a BBQ prong. 'Sorry, sorry, didn't mean to', shouted one of the local kids as he ran up to them. Rosie sat up to find herself covered in sand from her face down to her toes. Her dad extended his hand and helped Rosie to her feet.

'How does it feel? Are you okay?'

Wait! At this point I'm going to stop writing and just make it perfectly clear that this is not one of those poorly planned books where the whole thing turned out to be a dream! Goodness no, can you imagine the stick I'd get? – Anyway, carry on.

'Yes, I'm okay, thanks. Where's Pheebs?'

'Phoebe? She's over there, playing with the other...' Her dad was looking around, scanning the beach, trying to locate his youngest daughter as if he were one of those radar dishes that spins around in circles.

'That's odd', he said, 'I could have sworn she was'.

'Dad! When's the food ready?' Pheebs interrupted, running up next to them both from the sand dunes. 'I'm so hungry, it's been a long day'.

The girls exchanged looks for a moment, both of them swimming with emotion. Rosie opened her mouth to speak, unsure of what to say. She spoke to herself, 'Could it have been true? It must have been. How did Pheebs just appear like that? She must remember. I'll just ask her'.

'Right now – c'mon, let's go eat. I'm starving'. Their dad swooped down and grabbed Pheebs around the legs, hoisting her up onto his shoulders and grabbing Rosie's hand. He led them off back to the BBQ area. The other kids and parents were doing the same, loading sausages into buns and laughing as the odd one rolled off into the sand.

Rosie and Pheebs sat themselves down on a rug and ate their food in silence, keeping their eyes down to avoid any contact while they mustered their own thoughts. Soon enough, Pheebs was gathered up by her friends and went off to jump the waves.

Rosie's mum approached her. 'Rosie, I'm going to head back home and get some washing done for tomorrow. Do you want to come with me or stay here?'

'I'm okay here, thanks', Rosie replied.

'Oh, really? I thought you wanted to watch that YouTube thing you like'.

'It's okay, I've changed my mind'. She darted up and ran down to the seashore to join the wave-jumping session. Rosie grabbed her sister's hand and pulled her out a little deeper.

'Come on then, jump. Is that all you've got?' she yelled, clearing the little lapping waves with ease.

'I can take you any day', Pheebs replied as she leapt higher than her big sister, landing with a splash. All the neighborhood kids played for another few hours, running through the dunes, tossing a frisbee, and mingling with other kids they just met.

When the sun started to drop, the remaining dads packed up their stuff and grabbed their kids to head back home. The children were all tired and calmly helped to carry all the equipment back along the street with the school at one end and the beach at the other.

They all said their goodbyes as the various families tailed off to their own houses until Rosie and Pheebs turned into their road, walking a few steps behind their dad who was doing a heroic job of carrying way too many chairs, bags, and the BBQ.

'So then', Rosie quietly said. 'How was your time at the beach?'

'OMG, so it was real?' Pheebs replied, slightly less quietly.

'So you did go with me? – I mean, I knew it was real, but I didn't know that you knew'.

'Of course I knew! That mini dinosaur, and the fairies, gnomes, glowworms, all of it. It was all real!'.

'I can't believe it', said Rosie as they reached the door to their house. Their dad had already offloaded his stuff and was now being told off for walking sand into the house.

'What's the point of an outdoor shower, if you never use it?' came the distant plea from the girls' mum, who then followed up with, 'There's sand everywhere!' Rosie headed straight upstairs to see Pepper. The tail started wagging and hitting her bedroom floor long before she entered the room.

'Hi Peps – guess what happened to us? we had an adventure just like you said. I knew I'd heard you say that earlier, I just knew it!' Pepper responded by rolling onto her back expectantly, waiting for her tummy to get a jolly good tickling. 'Aww, you're so cute', Rosie said, obliging the old dog.

There was a call from downstairs. 'Girls – can you get washed and ready for bed, please?' Rather than waiting for their dad to repeat it 57 times, Rosie managed a reply the first time. 'Okay, will do', and with the most efficiency she had ever achieved in her life, proceeded to get washed, her teeth brushed, and into bed in record time. In fact, Pheebs did the same, it was all highly unusual.

'Do you mind if I sleep in your room tonight?' Pheebs asked her older sister. And she settled into Rosie's top bunk.

'Why are you in bed already?' mum asked them. The replies were, of course, different but alluded to both wanting an early night because they were tired. The sisters couldn't wait to get peace and quiet enough to talk about their adventure today but neither really knew how to start the conversation.

'Night, night', said their mum, closing the door.

'Night', said Rosie.

'Night', said Pheebs.

Rosie tried to distract herself briefly by opening a book she loved to read but today she couldn't' seem to loose herself in a fictional world. Pheebs noticed Pepper sitting up and staring out of the window she wondered what the dog might be thinking about.

There was silence as they both lay there, eager to speak Pheebs drew in a breath, about to ask Rosie if she thought they could ever go back.

Before she had the chance, the silence was disturbed by a startling, high-pitched voice.

'You thought you could hide your socks from us, did you?'

The girls both sat bolt upright as a flash of colour appeared in the corner of the room. One by one, they saw the sock stealing gnomes hop into the bedroom through the window.

'This time, there's no escape!' proclaimed Booey as the gnomes lined up on the floor.

'Uh oh', Rosie said. The sisters exchanged a glance. 'Here we go again'.

The End

For now...

Printed in Great Britain
by Amazon

37110323R00079